D1208237

YOU LEFT ME NO CHOICE   1

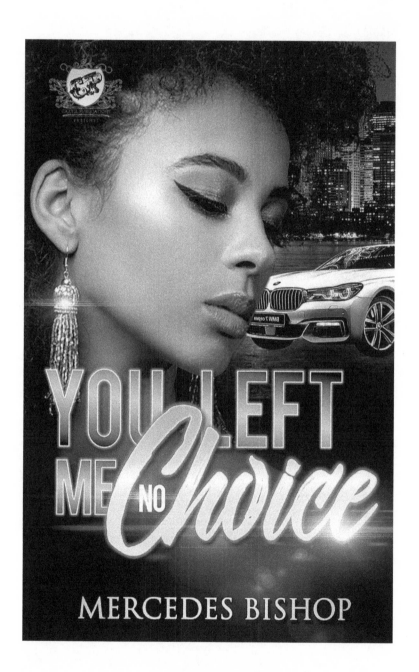

YOU LEFT ME NO Choice

MERCEDES BISHOP

CHECK OUT OTHER TITLES BY THE CARTEL PUBLICATIONS

4   BY MERCEDES BISHOP

YOU LEFT ME NO CHOICE   5

WWW.THECARTELPUBLICATIONS.COM

BY MERCEDES BISHOP

YOU LEFT ME NO CHOICE

BY

MERCEDES BISHOP

ISBN 10: 1948373130

ISBN 13: 9781948373135

Cover Design: Book Slut Girl

First Edition
Printed in the United States of America

BY MERCEDES BISHOP

What Up Fam,

I hope you all are safe and taking good care of yourselves. This pandemic is still not a joke, despite the government trying to open back up. If you don't have to be out, stay home. I believe the second wave will be worse than the first so please proceed with caution.

Now, onto the book at hand, *"You Left Me No Choice"* is a drama filled story that will keep you engaged from start to finish. We are so proud of Mercedes, who had a goal, took T. Styles' writing class and finished her novel! What an amazing accomplishment. If you love the books The Cartel Publications publishes, you will definitely be as proud as we are to add this one to your collection.

With that being said, keeping in line with tradition, we want to give respect to a vet or new trailblazer paving the way. In this novel, we would like to recognize:

GOD

I had to give it to God for the second book we put out in a week because He is worthy. In the good times, and in times of despair, God is able! Thank you, God for your grace and mercy. Thank you for keeping us protected and provided for and continuing to be a fence for our lives and the lives of our families. Continue to let us hear you and keep us faithful and blessed. We ask these things and all things in your son Jesus' name. Amen.

Aight Fam, I love ya'll and will talk to you again soon!

God Bless!

Charisse "C. Wash" Washington
Vice President
The Cartel Publications
www.thecartelpublications.com
www.facebook.com/publishercwash
Instagram: publishercwash
www.twitter.com/cartelbooks
www.facebook.com/cartelpublications

Follow us on Instagram: Cartelpublications

#CartelPublications

#UrbanFiction

#PrayForCece

#God

#YouLeftMeNoChoice

BY MERCEDES BISHOP

BLOODY WEDDING PARTY

We tried, we all tried.

But more things turned out wrong than right. Still, we stood in line, with fake smiles plastered on our faces. Especially me, standing next to Devon as his female best man. Even though I was in physical pain, I was willing to do my part, after all he asked. And at the end of the day I knew this marriage wouldn't last.

Too much had happened.

Too much was still happening.

Don't get me wrong, everything was beautiful. Love was placed into the ceremony. The bridesmaids wore emerald green dresses, the groomsmen in black suits with cranberry ties and the bride in a beautiful off-white gown speckled with crystals and pearls.

But what about two hours ago?

And what about the audience?

They weren't stupid. They all knew there was another part to the story. It was physically written all over our faces. Literally. My eye was black and painted over with a lot of foundation.

Brooklyn, Devon's other best friend, sported a busted lip. Jamie, his wife, who he was divorcing next month, had a gash over her forehead as she stood in the bridesmaid party.

And then there was the bride and groom, Devon and Miracle who although they were reciting vows, did so with malice in their hearts.

Yep, the crowd knew there was a story. But they didn't know the details. Besides, we had no intentions on telling anyone.

But I'll tell you. How else will I relieve myself of so much pain, irritation and hate? So, let's start at the beginning.

CHAPTER, ONLY THE BEST WILL DO

1

THE PAST

MIRACLE

I hadn't taken a bath in 48 hours and I was sitting in the doctor's office, preparing for my pap smear. I'm not normally a nasty bitch. Not physically anyway. It's just that things had been rough lately and I barely had time to shower. So, I resorted to running in the house, washing my hot spots and splashing on perfume.

Yes, now that I think about it, that was a bad idea. But hindsight doesn't help the future does it?

My life was full. I was having a wedding in a month, after having been in love with my friend for over five years. It didn't matter that he wasn't in love with me. Most people who are married fall out of love within the first year anyway.

Men are funny that way.

They think you don't know when things have changed. That you can't tell the hate on their faces as they look at your body when your back is turned. Or how they take secret phone calls in their cars that last for hours when you aren't around.

Nah, I knew months ago he fell out of like with me.

And so, I had to prepare.

People may say I was being deceitful, but you can say what you want. At the end of the day I always thought in advance. And that wasn't changing now. It would never be changing.

Plus, it wasn't like being with me wasn't an upgrade. I owned a lash shop in D.C. My car was paid off and I was tucking a little money aside for the house of my dreams. And trust me, the vision I had didn't call for some cheap ass hand me down. I went to an architect to have my home drawn up from scratch and I would do anything to see my dream realized.

"Ms. Jones, are you ready?" The nurse asked coming from the back room. She had a smile on her face that was fixed like one of these generic pictures on the wall. Like she couldn't be bothered to be genuine, so she resorted to fakeness instead.

Bitches are funny.

Still, even though she called my name there was one thing on my mind outside of my appointment. It's crazy, in less than a month I will be officially called, Miracle Ramsey.

And despite the condition of our relationship, I like it.

"Ms. Jones are you ready?" The nurse said more firmly. This time a scowl was planted on her face.

"I'm sorry, I'm coming now." I got up and walked toward her and into the patient room.

"You had your vitals done right?"

If she was referring to the temperature, weight and blood pressure check in the lobby the answer was yes. So, I nodded and took my seat on the doctor's table.

She handed me one of those cloth robes that I hated. You know the one with your entire ass hanging out of the back. "Can you put this on, open in the back? The doctor will want to give you a full examination. You're long overdue."

"Do ya'll have something else outside of this to put on?"

"Like what? Prada?"

"Wow." This bitch was being ignorant.

"Listen, it's been a long day. So, unless you want to be naked, wear the robe." She walked out.

That bitch did not have to get so smart! People kill me when they have jobs they don't really want. Don't take that shit out on me. If you don't like your place of employment, quit.

When the door was closed, I quickly got undressed and jumped in my blue gown, just as my phone rang. I could smell the sour scent of my vagina drifting up to my nose and regretted not rescheduling. Since my purse was across the room, I rushed over to my Neverfull MM, grabbed my cell and answered.

It was Jamie, one of my bridesmaids. "Hey, I'll be there in a second." I said, fingering my long braids so that they hung over the side of my shoulder. "I just got in the doctor's office and —."

"He's not here." She sounded out of breath but Jamie had a way of being extra so this could just be her tone for the day.

I frowned. "What you mean he not here?"

"I came over to get the money for your dress like you asked. But Devon not home. I thought you told him I was stopping by."

I looked down, and my stomach started flipping. I needed him to marry me and I needed it to be right. Was he actually about to change his mind like he did everything else in his life? "Is his truck out front of the house?"

"Nah. That's why I was calling to see if he was with you."

I shook my head as if she could see me. I mean, I can't believe he's doing this right now.

When I first told him he would marry me, he agreed that price was not a problem for our wedding or my dress. After all, it was the only way I would prevent my father from killing him. Mainly because he proposed in the past when he was drunk, and when my father got ready to foot the bill, he said he wasn't ready and backed out at the last minute.

I was not about to let him do that shit again. But by not giving her the two thousand dollars for my gown, he was fucking with my emotions.

"Miracle..."

"Uh, yeah. I'm here." I stared out into the doctor's office for a moment. I knew where he was, I just didn't want to admit it. My mood was precious these days and I had to protect it at all cost.

"What do you want me to do?"

"Go, I mean, go to *her* house."

She took a deep breath. "Are you sure? Because I don't want her tripping. You know how she is when—"

"Fuck you mean am I sure?" I threw my hand up. "Because you and I both know he's there. So, go get him!"

The doctor walked in and grabbed my chart. "Ms. Jones, it's good to see you again." He didn't mean it. I was always in here about something going on with my cooch so I'm sure he was probably tired of seeing it.

"Miracle, what are you doing?" Jamie said.

"One minute." I smiled and directed my attention to the call. "Go to her house like I said."

"I don't want to, Miracle."

"Don't fuck with me." I pointed across the room, but it looked like I was pointing at him. "Get over there now."

"Excuse me?" He said.

"Not you." I smiled again. And now just like the nurse, I felt fake. "Talking to a friend."

"I need you to end your conversation."

Focusing back on the call I said, "I've been planning this for months and nothing will stop me. Especially not a person not doing her bridesmaid duties. Now go over her house and get the money before I snap."

DEVON

BY MERCEDES BISHOP

This shit was crazy.

I just finished hanging with my man Lambo and he hit me back about this broad I fucked one time who was trying to flex like it was a regular job between us. The whole thing about it was I hadn't touched her in a minute. Our last fuck had to be three months ago. So why was she flexing like it was different. Long before I said I would marry Miracle for the second time. But he sounded like he didn't believe me.

The thing about a lie is this. If someone puts one on you, you can tell what people think around you by those who believe it.

When my other guy, Brooklyn heard about this scat running around town lying he came at me on the immediate and was like, *'Fuck nah that bitch lying.'*

But not Lambo. He was all, *'Damn nigga, I thought you were about to settle down and shit.'*

Two different people, two different reactions. But I also knew if Miracle found out about this shit, she was gonna flex hard. Cause a scene and make me want to smack the shit out of her, even though that wasn't my thing. So, I hung up on Lambo immediately, Brooklyn hit me back.

"Now she saying you told her you want to be exclusive." He said.

"Yeah, I heard about that shit too," I said to Brooklyn, as I drove down the street in my red pick-up. "Bitch is weird. If she keeps at it, she gonna have problems. Shit sensitive as fuck 'round here."

He laughed a bit long. "I know it. You want me to go over her crib and tell the bitch stop lying?"

"Nah, man." I chuckled. "If anything, that'll make her buckle up even more. The last time I saw her I threatened to fuck her up and she got all extra loud. Like she was trying to get a nigga locked up or something. I'll see her when I see her."

"My nigga, please don't go over that girl's house yourself. The last thing you want is Miracle finding out. I ain't got a problem on the pop up if you want me to handle it. Just let me talk to this bitch and —."

"I said I got it. Trust me."

"Your burial. Where you headed?"

"To Tammy's." When my phone beeped, I looked down and saw it was Jamie. "Fuck."

"What?"

"Your wife calling me again."

"That's cause you ain't give her the money for the dress for Miracle. I'm sick of her bringing it up and shit."

"I ain't give her the money cause I ain't have it to give." I shook my head.

BY MERCEDES BISHOP

"Then tell her that."

"You always think shit is simple."'

"I'm not saying all that. But having my wife hunt after you is foul."

Now I was the one laughing. "Oh, so now you wanna be a model husband and shit?"

"What I do to my wife and what other niggas do to her is two totally different things."

I really didn't feel like talking but he had a point. There was no use in my dodging Jamie. "Let me answer right quick. Hang on."

"Cool."

I hit the button. "What's up, Jamie?"

"What you doing today?"

I shook my head. Sometimes she did this thing where she beat around the bush instead of saying straight out what she wanted. It was an annoying ass trait. "I'm fine. What do you want?"

"Devon, Miracle is mad." She said with a lot of energy. "And I don't need all that right now."

"So why you got your foot at my neck about her?"

"Because you playing games that's why! Where is the money?"

"I'm not playing games. I just been having a lot of shit on my plate that's all. It's not really intentional."

Miracle knew she could pay for this fucking dress herself. I was barely making ends meet. But she was stingy as fuck and claimed broke more times than not. I believed in my heart she had a stash too. But was dead set on seeing me sweat.

"Well it feels that way." She paused. "Where are you right now? Wherever you are I can come by to scoop up the money."

"What money?"

"Devon!"

I laughed. Sometimes I liked fucking with her. "Listen, tell Miracle to relax. It ain't like we getting married tomorrow."

"And what does that mean?"

"It means she got time to pick up the dress."

"Devon, she gonna be —."

"I'll hit you back later, Jamie."

"But —."

"Just tell her I'll give her the money later." I hung up and switched back over. "Fuck, man. I need to catch a break with some paper for real. Miracle not gonna let this wedding shit go. Not this time."

"You ain't lying."

I took a deep breath.

Brooklyn sighed. "What you say earlier?"

"About what?"

"You goin' over Tammy's house?"

This nigga was so worried about my friendship with Tammy it was strange. "You got right back to it huh?"

"Because you stay tripping off her that's why."

"Ain't about tripping off of her. I just can talk to her about some shit I can't with niggas that's all."

"You sound dumb as fuck, D."

"How you figure?"

"The only female you should be—."

"Hold up, because this been bugging me. What is your thing with Tammy anyway?"

"I ain't got no thing."

"You sure about that?" I asked. "Because every time I bring her up, you be tripping."

"I'm just looking out for you. She got a nigga. And if she was my bitch, I wouldn't want her keeping no time with you that's all."

"Do me a favor, don't worry about what I got going on over here." I paused. "Let's just do that from here on out."

"Yeah, whatever, nigga."

When I hit Tammy's street, I saw some activity that was out of character at this time of night. "What the fuck?"

"What's wrong?"

As I pulled up in Tammy's driveway, I saw a yellow and white catering truck. It was obvious she was throwing a party, but I don't recall getting an invite. "Tammy tell you about a party?"

He laughed. "You playing right?"

"Nigga…"

"Nah she ain't tell me!" He said. "If she ain't tell you, she definitely didn't tell me." He laughed in a way that annoyed me.

I parked behind the catering truck. "Well she got something going on. I'ma hit you back though."

"Wait, you still meeting me down the bar, right?"

"Yeah but let me find out what's up with Tammy first. I'll get up with you later." I eased out.

TAMMY

I was having bad heart palpitations. It always happened when I was under pressure. At the end of the

BY MERCEDES BISHOP

day I was having a party for friends in six hours and I was nervous that things wouldn't end well.

Everything had to be perfect.

The food.

The mood.

I even saved a few bucks from my $14.00 an hour job to have it catered. I was even concerned about the smell being pleasing. To prove my point, I cleaned the bathroom three times since this morning and every time I used it, just to keep that fresh smell. I also burned vanilla scented candles so that people would be hungry and encouraged to eat snacks.

I wasn't a dirty housekeeper. It's just that, well, tonight was special.

Me and Carson had been kicking it for six months, but I never got to meet a lot of his friends. Whenever I asked him to tell me more about them, it was like he was guarded and tried to keep me away. It took a while for him to tell me the real reason he didn't want me to meet them and when he finally did, I was a little hurt.

"My friends kinda judgey." He said. *"I'll let you meet them when I can make sure we gonna be together."*

"So why they judge people?" I asked.

He shrugged and said, *"Because the last girl I dated was fucking her neighbor. I met the man, shook his hand and everything. I ain't no soft dude, but I'd be lying if I didn't say it took me out for a while."*

After I realized why he didn't want me to meet them, I wanted to prove that I was in it for the long haul. I cooked for him. Cleaned for him. Even ran errands that I knew he couldn't always care for so he would let them know. I didn't mind. Besides, everything about Carson was perfect. He was tall with a butter cup complexion and light brown eyes that made my pussy jump every time he looked my way.

But it was the way he held me in his arms, like it was the first time, that had me knowing he was the —

KNOCK. KNOCK. KNOCK.

What the fuck? Why were the caterers knocking? I told them I was leaving the door opened so they could bring the food inside.

When I walked to the door, I was irritated when I saw Devon on the other side. "What are you doing here, Devon?"

He pushed the door in stepped inside. "So, this how you do me?"

"Leave me alone and stop acting like your father."

"Don't refer to me as my father. Ever."

He hated his father and I never knew why. The only thing I did know was that they didn't have a

28   BY MERCEDES BISHOP

relationship and that at one point it was Miracle who tried to get them together. And then suddenly she stopped. I guess she realized she was barking up the wrong tree.

Slowly Devon walked to the food table and then the condiment table, before turning around to look at me. "I mean, fuck is all this about? You know I got the truck and—"

"Devon, what do you want?"

"I wanna know why you having a party without me?" He threw his hands up like I violated or something.

I closed the door and walked to the kitchen. I had so much to do so talking to him was annoying. Of course, he was on my heels as I moved throughout the house.

I would be lying if I said I was surprised he popped up over here without an invite. At the end of the day I been knowing Devon my whole life. We basically grew up together, literally in the same house. I was in foster care for one year before he moved in and started driving me crazy.

Number one, he was clingy. My friends at school couldn't understand why he got on my nerves because to them he was cute. I mean, I guess you can say he's fine, although I don't look at him like that. At the same time, I get the attraction.

He's about Carson's height, dark skin with short hair that curls up when wet. But Devon's also spoiled and a troublemaker who sometimes wants to take me with him. It's because of him I'm on probation for fighting and I can't count the number of times I got locked up fucking with Devon.

The first time happened when we were in the movie theater. It was a group of us. We liked going together everywhere and I enjoyed his company, I can't lie. All I know is that before Carson we couldn't do anything without each other. Think about me, Devon, Miracle, Jamie and Brooklyn all going to see a movie after leaving a bar. We were out of order. Loud. Dumb and we thought it was funny.

The thing is, everybody could handle their liquor but Devon.

So, when a lady in front of us asked us to be quiet, instead of respecting her, he goes off and ruins the movie for everybody by yelling and screaming. We left after being threatened with our lives by everyone trying to enjoy the movie. I thought that was the end of it. But when we got outside, he showed us the lady's purse.

How he picked it up, we still don't know. All I know is while we were outside, she must've noticed. So, a few minutes later she and her boyfriend ran out ready to fight. And who does she want to swing on? Not Miracle, who's 5'7 and sexy physique in the darkness of the movie theater, mirrors mine. Or Jamie who's a little shorter than the both of us.

Not even the person who stole her purse!

She comes for me.

Don't get me wrong, I got the best of her when we finally went to hands. Besides, where I'm from I'm used to fighting. She wanted the drama and she got what she ordered. I even sliced her face with a box cutter and everything. But I also got two months in jail and had to pay a fine for something Devon did. And instead of manning up and at least paying bail, he didn't even put up the cash. It was only after I threatened to never talk to him again that he gave me every penny owed.

But trouble didn't stop there.

A few months after that, Devon had gotten into a fight with Miracle and wanted to go out to "relieve stress". I knew I should have stayed home, but once again I let him pull on my emotions and before I knew it, I was in my car on my way to him.

Hours later, after leaving another bar, he gets into a road rage incident with a couple. When the guy slowed down and pulled out a gun, aiming it our way, I pulled out my .22 and shot up his car. It wasn't until the police came that I found out it wasn't a gun that the driver was aiming after all. But a black brush which he was swinging our way. I hated myself for believing our lives were in danger and choosing instead to act so quick.

So, at the end of the day Devon made me worse and I couldn't get away from him. That is, until I met Carson when I rented his house, this house. The thing was, it was Devon who saw our connection first since he was with me.

"You know you gonna be with him, right?" He said as we looked at one of the two bedrooms in my rental.

"What...nah, shut up." I turned on the sink. Truthfully, I was blushing and trying to hide it since Devon analyzed everything I did.

"Trust me. I ain't never see you light up like that for nobody."

"You seeing things, Devon"

"Maybe. But I don't think I'm wrong. That's gonna be your dude."

He was right. A week after I signed my paperwork to rent my house/apartment me and Carson had been together nonstop. Because of our newfound bond I pushed back on the time I spent with Devon. Originally, he claimed to want the best for me since we were friends. But as time went on, I was certain he was jealous.

But I didn't care. Because without spending every waking day with Devon, my life was peaceful and drama free. And it felt good.

Still preparing for the party, I grabbed the beer from the fridge and placed them in the ice chest on the floor. "I don't have to tell you everything I do, Devon."

"You sound crazy."

"I'm serious. You're not my man."

"Don't say stupid shit out your mouth, Tammy."

"You always thinking somebody moving on in life without you. Anyway, it's not that kind of party. If it was, I would have invited you over. You know that about me."

"Fuck that mean? Not that *kind of party?*"

"So, you really came over to fight?"

He rolled his eyes. "Whenever I have a party even if it's only two people, I invite you. But you moving like — ."

"Them whack as get togethers you be throwing at your house ain't no party, Devon!"

He backed up and held his chin like *Wee-Bey* from *The Wire*. "Oh, so you gonna front like we don't be having a good time at my crib?"

"It ain't about having a good time. It's about building a future. And I want to build one with Carson." I grabbed a few bottles of vodka from the freezer and placed them on the counter. "Like you doing with Miracle. I mean, I thought you were happy for me. At least that's what you said."

He took the Hennessy from my hand and stepped in front of me. I hated when he came so close because he...well...I don't know...it felt weird. In a way I can't explain. I felt immediately uncomfortable.

"Even if we do build a future, you gonna always be in my life. Like we promised each other when we were kids. And anybody before or after Miracle gonna have to understand. Can you say the same?"

I stepped back and looked away. "I'll call you tomorrow."

"Oh, aight," he said before walking out with an attitude.

BY MERCEDES BISHOP

DEVON

I was back in my truck, on the way to meet Brooklyn at the bar. I hit his phone to let him know I was on the way. I was so mad my head was rocking. This new nigga was causing problems. "Listen, order me a Corona and a shot of tequila."

"Why you sound mad, nigga?"

"I don't feel like playing."

"How I'm playing when I asked you a question? Sounds to me that you let Tammy's lil ass fuck you up again."

I wiped my hand down my chin. "I wanna, man, I feel like making moves on the nigga Carson. And I'm trying to calm down."

"What moves?"

"All I'm saying is somebody may have to hit Carson's head. And I'ma leave it at that for the minute."

I made a left on the street and then an immediate right.

"Is that somebody you?" He asked me.

"I'm just talking, man." I leaned against the window.

"Well don't say shit to me you don't mean." He said. "If you need serious moves made, I'm with it."

"Yeah, I know."

CHAPTER, CHANGES
BREAKS BONDS
2
DEVON

After kicking it with Brooklyn for a while I went home. And for real, I wanted to walk back out the room. We were supposed to be turning down the bed, but all she wanted to talk about was that fucking dress. And to be honest I was still kind of salty about Tammy not inviting me to her party. To me, we were better than that and I couldn't get it out of my mind.

The way I was feeling the last person I had time for was Miracle. But that didn't stop her from wanting to fight.

"You don't care enough to me, Devon."

"I'm not gonna do this with you."

"Do what? Tell me why you didn't come up with the paper for my dress? Do you even care how I look at our wedding?"

Damn she was blowing me. Every fight had to be knock down and dragged out and I was sick of it. "What you want me to do? Pull the money out my ass?" I yanked the sheet down on my side and slid inside the covers.

"Is the cash in there?" She slipped in the bed on her side.

"Stop playing with me, yo." I pointed at her.

"Devon, we getting married in a month." She pulled the covers up. "And it's important to me that the day is special. The pictures too."

"Why, so you can put it on social media for all them fake ass bitches?"

"I want the world to see our union." She sighed deeply "Do you even understand how a wedding is a girl's special day?"

I didn't. But she was searching for an argument and I wasn't going to give it to her. In my opinion if two people are together what difference does it make what everyone else sees? But that wasn't the case with Miracle. She was serious about having this long drawn out ceremony.

"You know I care how you look." I really didn't.

"Then why I feel like I want this on my own, Devon?"

"There you go hunting for a fight again."

"Do you even love me?" She asked.

I sighed.

Don't get me wrong, next to Tammy, Miracle was also my good friend, but she was so heavy. She claimed I asked her to marry me the second time and to be honest, I don't know that I did. The day was so cloudy.

All I remember was that we were out with the squad bowling the night before. The spot had some drink specials and I hit the credit card a bit hard. It started with the watered-down shots but then the bartender said Tito's was on special and so we moved to them instead. The next thing I remember I woke up and she was smiling.

"Fuck wrong with you?" I asked, yawning and stretching in bed. *"And why you got that dumb ass look on your face?"*

"I'm excited!"

I shrugged. *"Okay. But why?"*

"I thought you would never ask and finally you did." She hugged me tightly. *"You don't realize how happy you made me!"*

My eyebrows rose. *"Miracle, my temples are thumping. I got a hangover. So, I'm sorry. If you want me to know what the fuck you talking about, you have to say more than that."*

"You asked me to marry you."

"I did?"

"Ahn, uhan, Devon. Don't play games."

"I'm not!"

"Then why it looks like you want to take it back?" I could tell she was about to start crying.

"If I asked you to marry me, I mean, I guess, that's what it is."

And that was all she needed to run with this marriage shit.

She didn't care that I didn't have a ring. She didn't even care that I was having second thoughts in the beginning. She took it on the chin, bought her own ring and made all the plans. To be honest I was relieved I didn't have to come out of my pockets. Especially for something I didn't believe in. She only asked one thing from me.

To buy the dress.

And my stupid ass said yes.

"You not in this on your own, Miracle. I been told you that. So, stop making things strange between us."

She sniffled and wiped her nose and eyes. "Okay, well, um, what about my dress? You still gonna give me the money or not?"

"Like I said, I don't know about that part. Shit is a little hard for me right now. I'm not a rich nigga."

"I'm not with you for your money."

"Then what are you with me for?" I pulled the covers up and lie on my back. "I don't want to say it but, uh, maybe you should ask your father."

She glared at me. "Devon, are you serious?"

"Yeah."

"You really don't want me to do that. Because you and me both knows he wouldn't give me money unless I was dying. Even then he would probably want it back."

"Then I don't know what to—."

RING. RING.

I hopped out of bed to get my cell phone. It was Tammy. "I'ma take this right quick!"

"But we were talking."

"I be right back!"

I was already out the door when she yelled at me from the back. "Tell that bitch I said hi!"

When I walked into the kitchen, I tried to calm down and answered the call. "How was your little party? Was it better without me?" The moment I said it I felt stupid but like all things, it was too late to take it back.

"Boring." She said.

I laughed and for some reason, it made me smile. "Stop playing."

"I'm serious. It wasn't how I planned it. To be honest you should be glad you didn't go."

I hopped on the counter. "Well, um, is it over?"

"Pretty much. Carson out there talking to his friends now about football. And you know me, I'm not into all that shit."

I hopped off the counter and leaned against the refrigerator. For some reason I couldn't get comfortable when I was talking to her. "Maybe you should learn football. Dudes like that kind of shit, know what I mean?"

"Nah, I'm good."

I heard some people laughing in the background. "Tammy, niggas don't care a whole lot about you liking their friends. I mean, you don't have to work overtime trying to impress them."

"So, you don't care if Miracle likes me?"

I thought about how I ran out of the room just now and smiled. "You got it. Point made."

MIRACLE

It was about to rain, and I started to turn around, knowing my conversation would not end up well with my father.

"Daddy, I don't know what to do." I said as I followed him as he emptied out the quarters in the machine.

My daddy owned ten laundromats in and around Washington D.C. and was doing well for himself. But when you saw him, he was so mean looking and big, about 6'5 to be exact, that you would assume he was doing anything other than legitimate business, but you would be wrong.

"I don't know what you want me to say, Miracle. At the end of the day you need to leave him alone." He said dumping quarters into a money bag.

"But I can't."

"Why?"

"I have my reasons."

He shrugged. "So why you telling me? You won't take my advice. You won't listen. What exactly are you hoping?"

"I don't know, maybe that you would at least try to make me feel better about my life."

"I don't like the boy. Period."

"I know."

"Never have. The only thing you'll hear me say over here is to leave him alone. The day you wanna do that, will be the day I help. With everything you need. Outside of giving you money."

"Why is that, Daddy?"

"Because you have to make your own way in life. If I gave you money, then you would look to men to continue the tradition. And I don't want that."

"But I won't be down long, all I need is —."

"Don't start with me right now, Miracle." He waved over one of his men. "Take this out. It's in the way." The man lifted the quarter filled bags and my daddy walked to the back.

Once we were in his office, I sat in my favorite chair, an old white leather recliner in the corner. He sat behind his desk and took a deep breath while looking around. The one thing about my father is he always seemed annoyed.

"The reason I'm coming to you, I mean, even though you don't like him, is, well, I think he may change his mind."

He moved around some papers on his desk. "About what?"

"Marrying me."

He smiled. "Good."

When I saw the smile on his face, suddenly my blood boiled. My daddy had a tendency to treat everybody like shit, even me, but he usually came around. Today he seemed to take pleasure in my pain, and I hated him for it.

Irritated, I jumped up. "You know what—."

"Sit down."

I moved for the door. "Leave me alone."

"Sit the fuck down!" He yelled standing up. His knuckles brushed against his desk like an ape.

I sat down.

"I hate how you look right now." He took a deep breath. "Sad. Depressed. Despite my reaction, it really is tearing me apart."

I was shocked at his show of emotion. "Thank you, daddy. I, I know that was hard so I really—."

"You want me to kill him?"

I frowned. "Daddy, I—."

"You know the kind of man I am, Miracle. I haven't changed since you were a child. So, I ask you simply. Do you want him dead or not? Because if you do, I won't waste any time. "

Despite the threat on my fiancé's life, and me being afraid, I thought about how Devon didn't give me the money for my dress. I thought about everything I would have to go through when I later asked my father for it. I hated Devon for putting me in this situation because once again he was less than a man. Maybe he should die.

Instead I said, "No. Not for now."

BROOKLYN

As usual, I crushed these niggas in bowling and every last one of them were mad. Devon claimed he 'on't give a fuck but that ain't how he was acting. Like right now, he was balling up his face, kicking his feet and shit like that. At the end of the day I was still hitting 200 while he was yelling it's just a game.

"Where Tammy?" I asked as we sat down ready for the next round. I was cleaning my ball with a towel I brought with me.

"I don't know where she at to be honest." He shrugged. "She may come. She may not. Been brand new lately."

"Why you say that? I mean, she gets on my nerves every now and again, but she always comes out with us

BY MERCEDES BISHOP

to the alley." I paused. "Not to bring up the past but she usually comes to see me beat on that ass."

"I'ma really need you not to say that again." He drank the rest of his beer and turned the bottle up higher like more would magically appear inside.

I chuckled, grabbed the rubber band off my wrist and tied up my locs. "Nigga, it don't matter how I say it. The result is always the same. Your ass losing. You and me both know it."

He chuckled once. "Be back...gotta piss."

He walked away, just as my wife Jamie brought over my drink. The moment I saw the bottle, which was the wrong brand, I glared. Sometimes she drove me up a wall.

"Here you go, baby," she said extending the bottle with a weird smile on her face. Like she got it all right.

"Put it down." I lowered my head. "On the table."

She looked up at me, with them stupid ass eyes. I been married to this bitch for five years, and it's like she gets dumber by the second. Out of all the females I could've been with, why she have to enter my life?

"What's...what's wrong?" She asked in a shaky voice. "Did I, I mean did I do something wrong?"

"I asked for a Piper beer. What the fuck is this?"

"They didn't have that kind."

"Then you leave it there! You don't bring me what the fuck you want like I'm a pig."

My two other friends looked our way but then focused back on the lanes.

"I'll get it, baby." Her jaw trembled.

"I know you will. But before you go, come over here right quick."

"No...please—."

"GET OVER HERE!" I yelled pointing at the floor.

She shook her head no and I yanked her my way. When she was close enough, I punched her in the stomach. "Now, go make it right."

DEVON

"Nah, I gotta tell you something important," I said on the phone as I walked out of the bathroom in the bowling alley. "So, stop beating around the bush, Tammy. You coming or not?"

"Devon, if I get up there and you don't have anything to tell me I'm gonna be mad. I'm letting you know upfront. I don't—."

BY MERCEDES BISHOP

"This fucked up." I leaned up against the wall. "You know, I don't like having to do so much to get you out the house these days. We never had to do all this before."

"Let me guess, you 'bout to blame Carson again."

I shook my head and walked down the hall. "You must be reading my mind again."

"You talking to your girlfriend on the phone?" A cute brown skin chick asked me who was standing with her friends. Although her head stuck out, she didn't move her body so I could catch a good look at her ass.

I dropped the phone slightly to catch a better look. "Nah, she just my friend. Why you asking?"

She maneuvered around her girls and revealed her A cup titties. "First get off the phone so I can get to know you better."

I was about to respond when I heard Tammy yelling. I quickly placed the phone back on my ear. "What you say?"

"Devon, you and these bitches are gross. But just so you know I'm around the corner. See you in a second."

"Hurry up."

When I got off the phone with her, I was just about to see what was good with shawty when I saw Jamie doubled over as she walked toward the bar. I rushed in her direction instead. "What happened?"

She walked up to the bar and I was right behind her. "Nothing, Devon. Just, just leave it alone."

"You got a stomachache or..." I stopped in mid-sentence. I knew exactly what went down now. "He hit you again?"

"Just leave it alone."

Nah...I couldn't.

Instead, I could feel my face crawling up as I rushed toward Brooklyn. Don't get me wrong, I fucked with him hard. Besides, we had a business together and everything. But when it came to beating his wife, I wasn't with that shit.

"Fuck is up with you?" I asked rushing up to him.

He put the bowling ball on the rack. "What's wrong with you?"

"What I tell you 'bout putting your hands on that girl around me?" I asked pointing in the direction of the bar.

He glared. "What I do to my wife ain't none of your concern."

"None of my concern? Nigga, you punched her in the stomach."

"Again, that's my business. Not yours."

"You sure about that?" I asked stepping up to him.

"Devon, what's going on?" Tammy asked walking up behind me.

My gaze remained on Brooklyn.

"You better go see about Tammy and leave me and mine alone, Devon."

I gave him one more look and walked away.

DEVON

I was leaning on her dude's Porche talking to her about what went down inside. She drove it so much lately it was like it was hers.

When we first stepped outside, I was so mad I saw black. But within a few minutes I was relaxed and able to let the shit with Brooklyn go for now. She had a way of just listening without judging that I fucked with hard.

She never asked a bunch of questions, she'd just helped me work out solutions, even if I didn't know what I needed at the time. After rapping about Brooklyn and Jamie, we moved on to other issues.

She sighed. "I hear what you saying but the question is simple."

He nodded. "Okay...what is it?"

"What do you want?" She said. "I mean what do you *really* want?"

I shrugged. "I don't get the question."

She stood in front of me with her pretty self. It's crazy how she had the same body type as my fiancé and yet they looked totally different. She was stacked neat and right. "Do you wanna get married or not?"

"Why, you think I shouldn't?" I asked scratching my head.

"Nah, you not 'bout to do that shit to me." She said wiping her hair behind her ear.

"I ain't about to get you roped into nothing if that's what you think."

"Sure about that? Because you famous for looking for a way out of something and then blaming everybody else for why you changed your mind."

I chuckled once. "Did I ever do that to you?"

"No but—."

"If I never did it to you, then you shouldn't worry about it."

She took a deep breath and sighed. "How much is the dress anyway?"

I shrugged. "Not sure for real, but she asked for eighteen hundred."

She reached into her purse. "I don't have much, but I'll write you a check."

"Nah!" I yelled standing up straight.

She dropped her hand. "It's only two hundred dollars."

"I said no."

"Why, I know you'll pay me back whenever you get it. So, it's not a big deal."

"Tammy, I'm not about to have you buying my wife's dress."

"We friends, why not?"

That was a good point. So why did it feel so different? "For starters, she don't need money for real. You know Miracle's father—."

"Is the laundromat king, yes, I know."

"So, she'll be good." I paused. "If we got to, I'd rather borrow the money from Penny than anything else."

"Are you sure?" She smiled.

I looked at her a bit longer. She hated when I did this face to face. Not even sure why I was doing it to be honest. Maybe it was the way she had all intentions on coming to my rescue. I mean, I know I was broke as fuck, with running a food truck and having more overhead expenses than I realized but with her, shit just felt right.

"I'm positive. Trust me, I'm good. We good."

The moment I said that, Miracle pulled up in the parking lot all the way to the far end. I pretended not to see her but I definitely felt her presence across the way.

"Miracle, coming." She was about to look when I said, "Nah...let's just go inside." I moved to walk into the alley, but she wasn't following.

"Carson waiting in the car."

My stomach dropped. I was leaned up on the car and didn't even see him inside. I wondered how much he heard. At this distance more than likely everything. "Damn, I feel stupid. Why you bring him if you couldn't chill?"

"Because you said you had to tell me something important. And I was trying to be there for a friend."

"You could've stayed back if you were bringing him."

She grabbed my hand and let go. "I'll call you later."

"Don't bother." I walked off.

Miracle pulled closer to the front of the bowling alley just as Tammy was pulling off with Carson. To avoid being rude, she waved back but the gesture was clearly fake.

"Bitch," Miracle said to herself as she parked. "She fake as fuck."

When she was in a parking space, as she grabbed her purse and eased out, her heart rate kicked up when a pillowcase was thrown over her head and she was shoved into the back of a car. She gave up quite a fight, but lost the battle with a blow to the face.

At that time, she was immediately taken from the scene.

CHAPTER: WITH ME THERE'S ALWAYS DRAMA

3

TAMMY

The curtains were pulled back and the sun shined against Carson's face. He was so fine it was tough to look at him sometimes. Maybe it was my insecurity. I don't really know. But I always got the impression that things wouldn't last between us. It wouldn't be the first time I got things wrong with a man and that bothered me because I never really wanted to be alone. At the end of the day, I never trusted my own judgement.

When he moved a little in bed and I shifted, he opened his eyes. Smiling he asked, "What you doing, girl?"

I grinned. "Looking at you."

He smiled, closed his eyes and rubbed his belly. "Come on, man, you know I hate when you do that shit."

I kissed his lips and he opened his brown eyes. "Can't help it. You are so fucking perfect."

He shook his head and pulled me closer. While straddling him at first, I laid my head on the dips of his chest. It was only a matter of seconds before he got hard and entered my pussy. That shit was so slick and smooth, I almost didn't feel him slither inside.

Making love to him felt like a warm massage. If only he didn't wanna fuck so much.

Literally, before he closed his eyes, about thirty minutes prior, we just finished fucking. I don't know what it is with Carson, but we had to do it all the time and it drove me crazy.

As I remained on top of him, he moved in and out of me and it took another forty minutes before he came. Moaning loudly, he yelled, "Fuckkkkkkkkk. Damn that shit was right."

I eased off of him and laid on my side of the bed. "I was just trying to hug you. That went left quick."

"I can't help myself with you."

"I bet." When my phone rang, I grabbed it off the dresser. Staring at the screen my eyes popped open. "I gotta take this right quick."

He frowned. "Who is it?"

"Carson, stop."

"Why I gotta stop? I thought we got past you spending so much time with that nigga already. I mean, didn't you just see him at the bowling alley? Is it necessary to talk to him every five minutes?"

I hit the button to accept the call without answering. "It'll be quick. I promise."

"Make it quicker."

DEVON

Standing in my food truck, I just filled an order for a family of five. When I finally got Miracle on the phone, I turned to Brooklyn. "Handle things here for me. I'ma be quick."

"Who that? Tammy?"

I shook my head and walked out. I didn't owe him an explanation. Standing in the back of the truck, I said, "I'm surprised you picked up."

"You call me and that's what you lead with?"

I laughed. "Yeah…"

"Well I started to hang up. I hate when you call me and then make me wait."

She sounded the same but different. "My bad." I took a deep breath. "Anyway, I hit you because something's wrong."

"What?"

"Miracle ain't come home last night." I waved at the family eating the tacos we made them while sitting on a bench not so far away.

"Okay, so what's the problem?"

"I just said my fiancé didn't come home and you say what's the problem?" I shook my head. "I knew you could be insensitive but that's too much. Even for you. Are you cool?"

"I'm not trying to put off like it don't matter but ya'll fight all the time. Plus, she may be mad because you didn't give her the money for the dress. Sometimes girls just need a day away."

"Nah, this is…" when I saw Penny, Miracle's father, get out of his truck and walk toward me, I knew there was a problem. "I'ma hit you back."

"You starting to get on my —."

"I'll call you back." I stuffed my phone in my pocket and walked up to him. "Hey, Penny. Everything o —?"

"That my daughter?" He pointed at my pocket.

"What?"

"On the phone."

"Oh...no...it was...it was one of our friends."

"A female friend?"

I shrugged and nodded yes. "No."

"Yes or no?"

"No...uh...not a female. It was Brooklyn. Is something...like...is something wrong, Penny?"

He looked over at the truck and saw Brooklyn handing out food. He slowly glared because that meant he couldn't be on the phone. "I called my daughter last night. Was supposed to be stopping by to get the money for her gown. Seeing as how you failed to do your job and all."

"Sorry about—."

"Where is she?" He interrupted.

I shrugged. "I think she went to her salon."

"I went there first. They said she didn't have any lash appointments on the books. So, you wanna try this again?"

Fuck. What did he want from me? If I told him, we had a fight it would be over. "I really thought she was at work, sir. I don't know where she is now."

He stared harder. This man always rubbed me the wrong way. He never liked me. My mama said I ain't give him much reason to fuck with me, but I didn't give him any reason to hate me either.

"I'm gonna call her phone tonight, and you better hope she answers. Or else." He walked away.

TAMMY

Devon's apartment was so loud since all of us were there. He had this thing where he would ask a bunch of questions about a problem and then everybody would break off into huddles trying to figure out the best way to handle it. If we weren't working in groups, he would think we didn't care and use it as a reason to cut us off.

But with me, and the way I had things going in my life, I wanted order, especially since I hadn't been around them in a while.

Still, there me, Devon, Brooklyn and Jamie were, standing around the living room. Everybody had a beer in hand when I said, "I'm confused, what do you think happened to Miracle, Devon? Because your energy seems a little different than when we last talked on the phone. "

Devon wiped his hands down his face. "I…I don't know. That's why I'm asking ya'll for help."

I sat next to him when his eyes told me he was more concerned than he led off originally. "Okay, so when was the last time you saw her, Devon?"

"You must not be listening to the man." Brooklyn said to me.

I frowned. "How you figure?"

"Because the first thing he said was the last time he saw her was when she pulled up at the alley." He sat back in the sofa and yanked Jamie down, so she was propped directly under his arm like a pillow. "Sometimes I don't know why he still fuck with you."

"First of all, I've known Devon way longer than you ever did."

"Two years." He shrugged. "I give you that."

He acted like it was a competition when the both of us knew there was none. "You know, Brooklyn, the time me and Devon known each other actually makes up more since we lived together. And it ain't like I'm not listening to him. Just looking for clues that's all." I looked at Devon. "If you ask me, it has something to do with the bowling alley."

Brooklyn said, "You be tripping some—."

"She's right," Devon said cutting Brooklyn off. "I gotta replay in my mind what happened that night."

"Didn't much go on." Brooklyn said.

Devon rolled his eyes. "Some shit went down alright. Like me getting at you for hitting Jamie."

"He didn't hit me," Jamie said. "We got into an argument."

I frowned. Jamie had a way of taking up for Brooklyn after he beat her that annoyed us. It was so odd, at one point I thought she liked the abuse, until I saw her running down the highway in her panties and bra because she was trying to get away from him one night.

Devon shook his head. "Whatever...after I talked to Brook, I went outside and talked to Tammy."

I thought a little harder. "Wait a minute...you said some girls were there. What were they doing?"

"Just standing on the side of the wall." He shrugged. "Not really talking but not really doing nothing either."

"How many of them were there?" I asked.

Devon looked down. "I don't know. Maybe three or four." He rubbed his temples. "This just, just fucking me up now. I wonder if they were involved. Just seemed off that a female would come at me so hard."

"Don't worry about it, yo," Brooklyn said. "We gonna find out what the deal is."

"Right, she'll be okay," Jamie added.

"What I tell you about talking outta place?" Brooklyn said to her. "Huh? Did anybody ask you to talk?"

She shook her head no.

"Then shut the fuck up."

"I'm sorry." She looked down.

Hearing the way he spoke to her grossed me out. At the same time that was her life, not mine. Besides, if anybody came to the rescue, she would get angry. For real all I wanted to do now was help Devon. "Listen, I have it from here." I said to them both. "How 'bout ya'll go home? I wanna talk to Devon alone."

"Fuck no," Brooklyn said. "Miracle is like a little sis to me too."

"And I get all that but like I said, I gotta talk to him alone first."

He frowned. "You want me to go, man?"

"Yeah, let me kick it with T."

In full attitude mode, Brooklyn jumped up and stormed out, with Jamie behind him. "Hit me if you need something, Devon." He looked at me. "Since she wants us to bounce and shit."

When they were gone, the first thing I did was look at his place. Everything was junky and nasty, and it was like she'd been gone for more than one night. Miracle would never have stood for this mess. But I know exactly how it got this way.

When we lived in foster care together, he had a tendency of taking his clothes off when he got in from school and throwing them wherever they would land. Which was what he did over the course of her not being home. I knew I had to restore order if I was ever going to get through to him.

So, I tidied up as best as I could. After I cleaned up, I made him a meal from what was in the house. I ended up fixing chicken soup, rice and muffins. After he ate, I sat next to him and looked into his eyes. There was something I wanted to know but I didn't know how to ask.

"What is it?" He asked sipping soup.

"Did you do something to Miracle?"

He frowned and put the bowl down on the end table. "Why...why the fuck would you ask me something like that?"

I shrugged. "Because I gotta know."

"Listen, I got shit with me. Even if I wanted to fake like I don't, with you I can't. But there is no way in the world I would hurt her."

I believed him. "Okay, so she may have left you." I shrugged. "When me and Carson was pulling up into the parking lot she waved. Kinda had an attitude per usual. Maybe that made her mad enough to leave for a little while."

"I don't know, this feels different. And for real I'm about to lose my mind thinking about this shit. She didn't even hit her father."

"Where your cell?"

"In the car. The battery dead."

"Don't you think you might wanna charge that up? If she does call, how she gonna get a hold of you?"

"I'll get it in a minute." He looked at me long, hard and, well, wrong. "I know you different now, with your boyfriend and all. But I miss our bond."

"Different?"

"You know what I mean?"

I sat up straight. "Listen, I have to go, Devon. Just wanted to make sure you were good before I left."

He sat back deeper into the sofa. "Go 'head."

"You fine?" I asked.

"Does it matter?"

I got up and moved toward the door. I was already pushing the time limit to have dinner with Carson, and I didn't want him getting mad. And I knew Devon needed me during a time like this, but I had a man, and a life.

When I moved to the door I turned around. "I'll talk to you later okay?"

He nodded but didn't look my way.

I held the doorknob. "You gonna get your phone, right? So, you can charge it up in case I...I mean, she calls?"

He nodded again.

I pulled the door open. Everything in me knew I should be leaving but I couldn't go like this. It was almost impossible. And in the back of my mind I felt like he knew it too.

"Okay, Devon." I sighed and closed the door.

"Okay what?"

"Okay I'll stay a little while."

He smiled.

MIRACLE

I was lying in the trunk of a car in my own urine. What was going on? I mean, I knew I was somewhere next to busy traffic but didn't know where. I had to get out of here. I had to save myself. When I figured the coast was mostly clear, I grabbed my smart watch from my boot and looked at the screen.

I had ten percent battery and counting. It wasn't like I didn't try to get help before. I had already called the police several times, but because I didn't know where I was, and didn't have an Apple Watch, they couldn't find me.

After dialing Devon, a million times with no answer, I decided to call Jamie. My heart dropped when she answered. "Who dis?"

"Jamie, listen, listen, listen…" My breathing sped up so fast I couldn't get calm. I also had to keep my voice down, since I wasn't sure who could hear. "Jamie, I—."

"Who is this?"

"It's me, Miracle."

"Miracle! Where are you? We been—."

"Shut the fuck up," I said through clenched teeth. "Now listen, you have to find Devon. Tell him I've been kidnapped."

"Kidnapped? Are you serious?"

"Bitch, with this I don't play."

"Well why you ain't call Penny? Or the police?"

"You know my father don't have no phone. But I overheard the men say they left the info with somebody. You know where Devon is?"

"Yeah, he at home. Me and Brook were over there yesterday, and Tammy put us out."

I felt my face heat up. "Go get him! Tell him what happened. Now!"

CHAPTER, PAY UP AND LIVE

4

TAMMY

When I woke up, I was sleeping on the foot of Devon's bed and he was fast asleep. The plan was to stay for only an hour, but I was so tired I dosed off. When I grabbed my phone, just as I thought Carson called a million times. "No, no, no, no." I slipped off the bed and looked for my shoes.

Devon woke up yawning. "What's wrong?" He rubbed his bare chest. Why did he take his shirt off? We definitely didn't fuck.

"I'm not supposed to be sleeping over here, that's what's wrong." I found my shoe and dropped on the bed to put it on, before grabbing the other. "You should've woken me up. You said you would wake me up."

"I should've woken you up?" He pointed to himself. "Have you forgotten what happened to me last night? That I'm still trying to find out what's up with my fiancé?"

BY MERCEDES BISHOP

I did.

I looked back at him. "I'm sorry. I'll—." When my phone rang again, I answered. "Hello."

"Where are you?" Carson asked in a calm but firm voice.

My eyes widened. "I'm so sorry, baby. I, I overslept. And I know you were waiting on me so—"

"Overslept where?"

Here was the dangerous part. If I said I overslept over Devon's, he would definitely break up with me. I know for a fact he thinks something is up with us even though it is not. But If I said I overslept at my house; he could still get mad but at least he wouldn't have to think the worst. "At home. I'm so sorry."

"You're lying, Tammy. I went to your house and your car not out front."

CLICK.

"Fuck, fuck, fuck, fuck!" I yelled grabbing my purse.

"Where you going?"

"Just leave me alone, Devon! You really did it this time!" I ran out the door.

TAMMY

I was standing in front of a new house Carson was renovating. He had been at the property for a few days, so I knew where he was. I was about to knock when he came out of the door. The moment he saw my face, he was about to walk back but I ran after him. "Carson, please talk to me!"

He walked inside and I followed him. Stepping around a few men tiling the living room floor, I made sure to keep up my pace.

"Get out, Tammy."

"Please! I know...I know I lied but—."

"But what?" He stopped walking and faced me. "What have I ever done to you to make you feel like you have to lie to me? Didn't I treat you better than that? Weren't we better than that?"

I looked down. "You're right."

He started walking again. "Being right ain't helping me, Tammy." He walked to the bedroom and again I followed, closing the door behind us once we were inside. "It just means I chose wrong."

BY MERCEDES BISHOP

Throwing my purse on the filthy floor I took several deep breaths. "I know you think I'm like other girls but—."

"You just like them other bitches."

My eyes widened. For as long as I've known Carson, he never cursed at me. He was always easy going which was one of the reasons I liked him so much. So, what changed now? "Carson, I was with my friend Jamie."

He frowned. "Never heard of her."

"That's because you never wanna meet my friends."

"Nah, that's because the only person I hear you rapping about is Devon." He looked at me closer. "That's probably where you really were. Tell the truth. Put it all out on the table now."

"I wouldn't do that to you."

He frowned. "Do what? If it's a friend and you were there, shouldn't nothing be popping off to begin with. So, what would there be to do?"

My breathing increased and I felt myself on the verge of a panic attack. The last thing I needed was for us to be fighting each other. If we were going to work, we had to respect our bond. "Carson, I—."

"It's over."

My eyes widened and I reached for his hand. He pulled away. "Please, no, no, don't do this."

"Nah, this a good thing. Consider this my letting you go. That way you can be where you want to be."

I heard him talking but my stomach churned as he continued to speak. Don't get me wrong, we haven't been together forever. But being with him gave me hope. It gave me somewhere to be during the storm of life. And he was about to take it all from me. And I couldn't handle losing him.

I grabbed his hand and squeezed it harder when he tried to pull away again. "Don't do this."

He tried to walk off and I pulled him closer. My face nestled in his soiled shirt. Even in his work clothes he smelled good. Like a man who showered earlier but had gone on with his day in an effort to get the bag. Everything about him called to me and there was no one on the earth I had a connection with...*in this way*.

Yes, I loved my best friend Devon. But it ain't nowhere near the same. I would drop everything for Carson. I wouldn't drop everything for Devon. If I had to be without one or the other, it would be, well, Devon.

I think.

"I'm so sorry, for hurting you. For disrespecting you. I know you put a lot of love into our date last night and I treated you like shit."

He looked away. "Nah...it don't even matter. I'm—"

"But I promise, if you give me one more chance, I'll do anything, Carson. I don't care what it is just say the word."

He stopped trying to get away. "Anything?"

"Yes." I put my hand over my heart.

"I asked you to move with me to Atlanta next month. At first you said no. Talking about your friends need you. If you want to be with me, that's the move I'm making. Will you go now?"

I looked down. "But the wedding is—."

"After the wedding." He stepped closer. "I'm not a monster. But the next week I want us gone. No more playing games. If you wanna be with me, that's how you do it. So, what's it gonna be?"

BROOKLYN

Sometimes my wife acts stupid as fuck. Like she got a problem thinking straight. That's why I gotta beat her ass so much. I gave her simple orders. Told her to pay the cell phone bill with the food money because we were backed up and I wanted to make shit work. And what did this stupid bitch do? The exact opposite.

Now my cell phone off. Had it not been, I woulda never had to pull up over this nigga's crib. Which was some place I ain't want to be.

Taking a deep breath, I parked my car on a block in Washington D.C. You ain't venture over these parts unless you knew somebody. It could mean trouble for sure. I knew a few niggas and at the same time, I tried to steer clear of this scene. But today I had no choice.

I stepped out my car, looked around and knocked on the door of a rundown townhouse. When it opened, Berkley snatched me inside by the forearm. He was a big, black nigga who just got out of jail. In the beginning he was trying to lead the right life, until his baby mother took him for child support. When they gave him two months to come up with the money or go back to jail, he hit me.

And I had a plan for us both.

"Fuck is you doing over here?" He asked, scratching his beard. "I thought we weren't supposed to be seen together."

"My wife man, she…you know what, it don't even matter." I closed the door. "How shit moving?"

He dusted his thick bush back with his long fingers connected to ashy knuckles. "Before we get into all that, come get something to eat right quick."

"Nah, nigga, I can't stay for all—."

"Bitch ass nigga, come eat!"

I shook my head and walked back into the kitchen. Could I eat? Yes. But the place was nasty as fuck, I can't lie, and I dreaded having to put anything in my face in here. At the same time, I needed this nigga.

I pulled out a chair from the dirty table, dusted cat hair off the seat and propped down. The whole time this nigga smiling like he on some five-star shit. "What you want me to taste?"

"Not taste, eat. I made this recipe for—."

"Let me stop you right there." I threw a palm in his direction. "Devon ain't accepting no more recipes for the truck right now. When he do—."

"Nigga, just hear me out. Plus, people getting tired of eating the same old shit on that truck. I have it on good authority that it ain't a good look." He pointed at me. "Ya'll need variety. Shake things up a bit. That's where I come in."

I didn't have time for this. "Just give me what the fuck you got to eat so we can get down to business please."

He happily turned around and started scooping shit out of filthy pots. This man was a whole killa, and here he was trying to impress me with a meal I had no intentions on swallowing.

When he was done, he scooped two plates up and handed me one. Slowly he sat across from me. "Well."

I looked down at the plate. "What I'm supposed to do? Use my fingers?"

"You want me to clean one out the sink?"

When I saw a roach crawl out of it, I shook my head. "Nah. I'm good."

"Well eat."

I cracked half a smile and looked down. The meal consisted of eggs with a lot of veggies inside, some bacon and some bread looking thing. I scooped out the eggs with my fingers and was surprised at how good it tasted. At the same time, you couldn't say too much because he would be hounding me.

"Well?" He asked with a wider grin.

"I'm eating, nigga, damn." I said chewing carefully, to be sure I didn't taste bug legs.

He waited all of one second and said, "*Welllllllllll?*"

I exhaled. "Fuck, it's good aight?" I pushed the plate aside.

He leaned back with a grin on his face. "So, you gonna put a word in with Devon? Cause I got all kinds of recipes and shit like that."

"I be telling you that—."

"Listen, I'm trying to get off the streets. You know I got kids and shit, man. But I know cooking. And I know you look at my place and automatically think shit be nasty, but I feed a lot of people in this bitch and they don't always look out on the clean-up tip. So, I make do."

So why couldn't he clean up now? "I ain't saying—."

"Stop judging people and give a nigga a chance, Brook." That's all I'm saying.

I sighed. "I'll tell him about your recipes."

He clapped his hands together. "Good."

I looked around. "Now can you please tell me what's up?" I whispered. "You got her in here or not?"

"Yeah, she downstairs." He whispered. "I had her in the back of the trunk until I could run people outta here."

"You sure you not gonna have no niggas in and out of here right?" I asked leaning closer. "Because that's our money downstairs. They see her or set her free and we short. You gotta play smart."

"Trust me, ain't nobody coming up in here. I'ma clean up, get shit together and wait on the call."

"Ain't no waiting. You gotta put the voice box on and call for the paper yourself. I thought you did that already."

"I got you." He said. "Now you sure Devon gonna give us the money? Because I heard he ain't got no—."

"Not Devon. He broke!" I pushed the plate further away. This nigga wasn't paying attention. "You gotta hit Penny. We talked about this, man."

"I don't know about that nigga Penny."

My eyes widened. "Fuck that mean?"

"He a killer."

"Oh, so now that's a problem? Because the bitch was still his daughter when you snatched her." I squinted at him. Something felt off. "Why you feel a type of way all of a sudden?"

He glared. "What is it with you, Brooklyn?" He paused. "Huh? Ain't that your man's girl? Why you doing all of this?"

I sat back and crossed my arms over my chest. "My reasons are my reasons."

"That ain't what I asked you."

"Look, at the end of the day it's my business. But if you must know, all of my reasons revolve around money. Besides, you the one who called me and set all this off." I stood up. "Now put a call in to the nigga Penny so we can get this paper." I shook my head and walked out.

DEVON

My head been rocking all day long. It wouldn't go away. I done took everything I could from aspirin to Tylenol and nothing seemed to make me feel any better. I was about to pour some Henny down my throat when Brooklyn hit my cell. I reluctantly answered. "What?"

"You good, man?"

"Nah." I flopped on the sofa and rubbed my temples.

"Heard anything yet?"

"What you mean heard anything?"

"I mean…did she call and say something?" He paused. "Or is she back home? I'm just trying to get more info because we been worried like fuck about you on this end that's all."

I sighed. "I heard some voice messages from this weird ass number. But the shit was too gargled to make out." I shook my head. "I don't know where she is, man. Or what's going on. All I know is Penny bitch ass acting like I should have the answers when I don't."

"That nigga there always trying to punk niggas."

"How can I have the answers when she won't even reach out to me?"

"You know how Miracle is when she can't get her way. I wouldn't be surprised if she's posted up with another nigga just to see you rattled."

"I hope so." I sat deeper into the sofa. "But to be honest, it ain't looking good." I was just about to get up when Penny walked through the front door with two big ass niggas as if he wasn't intimidating enough. "What the fuck?"

"They asking for money?" Brooklyn asked.

"Asking for money? What...let me hit you back." I hung up and stood up. "What you doing here? How you get in?"

"You want me to walk back out and show you?"

I glared.

"Now sit the fuck down. We have to talk."

I sat.

"I got a call today, about my daughter."

My eyes widened. "Okay, well, is she, is she okay?"

"You tell me." He crossed his arms over his chest.

"I have no idea, man. I been hitting her phone and—.""

"She's been kidnapped. You know anything about that?"

I put my hand over my chest for some reason. Maybe because this man scared the fuck outta me or maybe it was the fact that my heart was pounding. "I promise, this the first I'm hearing of it."

"I'm gonna ask around on the streets. But if this is real, I'm bringing the money to you."

"Why would you do that?" I frowned.

"Because that was the directions."

Somebody was trying to kill me. Somebody was really trying to kill me. "I don't know nothing about all that, Penny. That's for real."

"If I find out you had anything to do with this shit, I'm killing you." He pointed at me. "You do understand this don't you?"

I nodded quickly hoping they'd get the fuck out so I could wrap my mind around what was just said. "Okay...okay."

"Now stand up. I want to give you something." The moment I did, one of the men stole me in the jaw. Now my headache went on ten.

CHAPTER, A NIGHT
WITHOUT THEM
5
TAMMY

This was so nice.

Carson had prepared a serious meal for me at his house and I can tell it was done out of love. And so, I put my phone in his bedroom, away from us so that he would know I'm serious about our relationship. That I'm serious about him. The man could cook too. He made fried chicken that tastes better than grandma's, red potato salad and asparagus with garlic butter. And when I finished, I sat back in the dining room chair and looked at him. Mostly in awe.

"Don't look at me like that, girl," he said sexily. "You gonna find yourself in a situation."

I liked the sound of that. "What you gonna do if I don't stop?" I leaned in and licked my lips.

"We done went two rounds already, lady. You sure you got another one in you? Because I'm game."

Actually, I didn't have another round. Like I said, Carson liked to have sex so much my pussy lips were raw to the touch. And at the same time, I was willing to do anything I could to prove that I'm with him.

So why couldn't I get my mind off my friend?

Me and Devon have always been there for each other. Through the good and bad times. And it fucked up my head that he was probably somewhere dealing with Miracle leaving him. Alone. But what could I do? I made the choice and I had to see things through, right?

"Let's sit on the sofa," I said. We did. "This feels nice." I continued as I nestled into his arms.

"What you want out of life?" He asked, readjusting his dick to the left. My tired lil pussy jumped. Maybe I did want him more than I realized sexually.

"You mean what do I want besides you?"

"I'm serious, Tammy. One thing I see about a lot of pretty girls—."

"Oh, so I'm pretty huh?"

"Nah, you beautiful." He winked. "But I'm serious. What I see about a lot of pretty girls is that they never really think about what they want. They ride off their looks and when they get to a point where it won't take them any further, they don't know what to do next. And I don't want that for you. So, what do you want out of life?"

He had me thinking.

He was right. I had a little job at a real estate company where I answered the phones, but most of my time before Carson was spent with Devon. Riding life. Not really having a direction. That's another reason I cared about Carson. He was well rounded, and I needed a grown man in my life.

"I wanna do what you do. I mean, I know there's a lot involved but that's a real dream of mine. It's one of the reasons I work at the company."

"What part interests you most?"

"Real estate. Selling houses."

He smiled. "You for serious?"

I positioned myself to look into his eyes. "Yeah, I mean, I don't know about getting that far into it, like rehabbing and stuff like that, but I wanna own homes and rent them out." I looked down. "But I'm not that smart. I ain't even finish high school so it will stay a dream."

He raised my chin. "You should go back. To school. At least get a G.E.D."

"Nah, it ain't that important."

"Come closer."

"I'm still sore."

He laughed. "Get over here."

I stood up and sat sideways on his lap. "Listen, you can have and be anything you want in life. Especially with me at your side. Don't ever stop excelling because you don't have an example. Or you don't see a way. Because I see the future even if you don't, Tammy. And it's bright."

My stomach flipped. "Wow. Nobody...nobody has ever said that to me."

"I want you to stop that shit too." He nodded. "When you talking to me, let your thoughts stay with me." He paused. "Okay?"

His eyes. Oh my God. "Babe..." I said.

"What up, girl?"

"I'm ready."

"Let me hear the words."

"I'm ready for the dick."

He smiled, lifted me up and carried me into the room.

TAMMY

Before fucking I lotioned up my body with shea butter and castor oil. Carson was a toucher and when his fingertips peddled over my body, I wanted my skin to be smooth to the touch at all times. I knew he was sleep because he was already snoring after the last round. So, I knew he would be out now. And that was a good thing because I wanted to shower again.

When I walked out of the bathroom, I was surprised to see him sitting up, with his back against the headboard. A red cup sat on my table and a blue cup was propped up on his. "I made you some tea." He said.

I touched my heart. "Awww, Carson…that's so cute. I thought you would be out for at least fifty minutes."

He patted the bed and I took off running before jumping next to him, nestling myself under the covers. He reached over on his table, past his cup and handed me a check.

"What's…what's this for?"

"Your start."

My heart rate kicked up and I sat up in bed. "Carson, I can't…I can't take…I mean, can…"

"If you're worried about me don't. I don't give money to people I don't care about. And I don't give any money away I can't afford."

When I looked at the check my breath was choked. It was for twenty thousand. "This seems like so much."

"It's not." He shrugged. "I'm gonna have my girl set up your LLC in Atlanta. And then you are going to live your dreams, Tammy. That's what I want for you. It's what I wanted for you since we met."

"Carson, I —."

RING. RING. RING.

It was my phone. FUCK.

He looked at my cell on the table and sighed. "It's after hours."

He was right. "I know."

"So, don't answer. We're still talking."

"But, I mean, I think it's Devon."

"It's always Devon. But if you answer that call, when you're in bed with me, I'm gonna think shit ain't real. Is that what you want?"

Of course, I didn't, and I knew he was right. Besides, the man had perpetrated the greatest act ever. He put money into me and my dream. So, I turned the phone off, and slid deeper into bed.

DEVON

I was sitting in my living room on the sofa trying to get a hold of Tammy. But every time I hit her line I would be pushed to voicemail. "Fuck." I tossed the phone on the sofa and dragged my hand down my face.

"Why you tripping off that bitch?" Brooklyn asked as he texted on his phone. "If she ain't answering, fuck her." He put his phone down.

"Can you stop acting like she some dumb bitch?" I got up and walked to the window and looked out. The streets were mostly empty, but I felt like someone was watching.

"All I'm saying is your wife is kidnapped and the only thing I'm hearing about is Tammy. Your priorities is a little messed up if you ask me."

"Fiancé."

"What?"

I looked at him. "Me and Miracle ain't married yet."

"You know what I mean." He took a deep breath. "You should readjust your focus. Anyway, what time Penny coming?"

"He should be on his way. I swear to God I don't feel like dealing with this nigga. Not now, not never to be honest."

"How much money they asking for?"

"One hundred thousand. They told him he had to let me drop it off and it's making it look like I'm in on this shit." I flopped on the sofa.

"Penny don't believe you involved. If he really did, you'd be dead."

I frowned. "Have you met this man? Ever."

He shook his head. "Like I said, if he really thought you had something to do with it, he would have dealt with you a long time ago. That man just wants his daughter back that's all."

"Yeah, well he going about it the wrong way."

"I'ma roll out then."

I frowned. "Why?"

"Because if he sees I'm here he gonna be extra irked. If he don't like you, you know he can't stand my food truck ass."

He walked over to me and I shook his hand. "Aight, I'll hit you later."

"Let me know what happens." He walked out and I sat back in my seat.

I gotta deal with this shit. Ain't no other way around it. But having my shawty snatched without my best friend felt different. I get her dude wanting to spend time but cutting her off from her people is cheesy.

I mean, what the fuck? I been knowing her way longer than him. Worse than anything, I'm mad that she letting him do this shit. She acting like we don't have history. Like I haven't been there for her when she needed me the most. I can tell you one thing straight up; I never turned my back on her.

Ever.

When I walked to the window again, I saw Penny's truck pulling up in the parking lot. It was a black extended Escalade with big ass tires to hold his wide ass frame. He climbed out the back, and his driver stood on the side as he walked toward our building holding a duffle.

I walked away from the window and paced the floor. "Fuck, fuck, fuck."

MIRACLE

I was lying in the basement on a blanket, inside of some raunchy ass house that smelled damp. Earlier in the day someone told me I would be going home. And when I asked when, I was kicked in the face. I took from that they didn't want me asking questions but that wouldn't stop me. I would just have to get smarter. After all, what was I going to do? Sit here and wait while people I didn't know held my life in their hands?

"Excuse me!" I yelled again. "Excuse me!"

Within a few seconds, I heard footsteps rushing downward. Before long, a man wearing a ski mask pushed the door open and put the gag back in my mouth. This time it was tighter. "Ouch, you hurting me."

"Fuck he leave the gag out for?" He asked as he tied it tightly.

Who was he?

"I'm hungry," I mouthed as I moved my lips. The words came out broken because of the position of the gag. "When am I gonna eat?"

"You gonna have to wait on the paper first. We not wasting no food on a dead woman."

"Paper from who?" I mouthed again. "My daddy?"

He walked toward the door.

"From who?" I mouthed louder.

He slammed it shut leaving me alone.

JAMIE

I had been sleeping all day after me and Brooklyn fought. I wish I knew what to say, what to do, to get him to stop being so angry. It all started last night when I was making dinner. My husband is particular. If we have fried chicken in the earlier part of the week, he won't want it again on Saturday.

All I asked was did he want fried chicken because he went on about how good it was. I thought he was hinting around breaking the usual way of preparing meals and I wanted to be sure. He yelled no before going on and on about how stupid I was. And how I couldn't remember the littlest details. All I wanted was to make him happy. It's all I've ever wanted.

In a way, I always seemed to annoy him. To make him feel like I wasn't trying my hardest. Technically I'm surprised he even chose me. I always thought he had eyes for Tammy. Of course, I'd never say it out loud.

I'm glad I didn't because now I know better. I think he hates her.

My marriage is on the rocks. He often talked about divorce. But I hated the thought. We go through shit but isn't drama passionate? That's how I feel anyway.

After being in bed all day I decided to get up. To prepare him a nice meal. I don't have any idea what he wants but I do know what we haven't had in two weeks. And that's homemade pizza from scratch.

So, I made up the bed and swept a little around our room. Cleaned up the kitchen using his favorite disinfectants and jumped in the shower. When I got out of the bathroom I paused when I heard him on the phone. Normally I don't sneak around but he sounded excitable, as if something was wrong.

So, I cracked our bedroom door open just a little more and eavesdropped.

"He's gonna meet you in fifteen minutes." My husband said. He was walking around the living room like he couldn't stay in one place for long.

"Yeah, man! Just…just make sure you're there to get the package." He paused. *"What you mean what am I gonna do? I'm gonna come by and park up the block in a rental. Because we definitely wanna stay low key in case they call the police."*

What was my husband talking about? His entire conversation and demeanor were suspect. If we were on better terms, or I cooked his food the right way, I may have felt comfortable enough asking him. But my job was to always make things easier not harder, so I had to fall back.

"I know, but don't bring Miracle." He continued.

My eyes widened. Don't bring Miracle? Don't bring her where? Wasn't she missing?

"I know what I said." He continued. *"But that ain't what we doing now. I'm changing the plan."*

I opened the door wider, but not enough to be seen. It felt like the door closed made it harder to hear.

"We gonna keep her until I say so. And if shit ain't good, we gonna kill her."

My stomach felt as if it dropped in my drawers. I couldn't be sure, but it sounded like, like he had something to do with Miracle's disappearance. This would kill Devon if he ever found out. It's killing me now.

At the same time, maybe Devon wouldn't be destroyed because he doesn't love her. If you ask me, I think he loves Tammy but neither of them knows. It would kill him because he has been friends with

Brooklyn for as long as I could remember. Devon was like his brother and this…this wasn't good.

"Nah, nigga! Ain't nobody give him them dumb ass recipes yet. Just do your job and keep an eye on our product."

I needed to tell somebody. But who? If I went to my husband to question him about what I overheard, he may be liable to act more violently. If I went to my friends outside of our circle, there was nothing to stop them from telling the world.

But there was no way I was going to keep this to myself. And I couldn't if I wanted to. I guess I didn't know my husband as well as I thought I did.

CHAPTER, YOU CAN'T LEAVE WHAT'S A PART OF YOU

6

TAMMY

I couldn't believe I slept this late. Normally I woke up around 8 o'clock in the morning but being with Carson felt effortless. When this man laid in the bed with you, you knew he wanted to be there. You knew he enjoyed being connected to you. I just wished I wasn't so damn toxic.

Because most of the time as I laid beside him, I kept wondering if Devon was okay. Sometimes I hated telling people about our friendship because they really didn't understand. My mother seemed to believe I'm emotionally connected to Devon because she fed me chitterlings when I was little. Said I developed a taste for what was bad for me. But that couldn't be further from the truth. I just, I just worried about him that's all.

And then there was the history we shared. When she wasn't around, and I was in foster care, Devon was the one who was always in my corner. He was the only person always in my corner. The man was always there and as a result, our bond was just different.

When I glanced over and saw Carson still asleep, I looked on my headboard and grabbed my cell phone. I turned it off in the middle of the night because I knew my friends would be blowing it up. I was the only one who seemed to understand how to dig us out of trouble, but I was in a serious relationship now and needed Carson to know it was real.

I sound like a parrot, I know.

The moment I turned on my phone it dinged repeatedly with voice and text messages. I hadn't seen it go off this much sense Miracle and Devon announced their wedding. I actually felt bad when he said they were getting married because for some reason I had a stomachache all that day and couldn't participate in any of the celebrations. The doctor said I was fine, but I didn't feel that way.

Scrolling through my phone, I noticed the first few messages were from a friend I hadn't spoken to seriously in about three months. I avoided her mainly because whenever we spoke, she was always crying about something not being good in her life. Like seriously, she was the only person I knew who always had a sad story.

The next message I read was from Devon and it simply read: URGENT.

He didn't give specifics but I'm pretty sure it has something to do with his fiancé. The next few text messages after that were the same coupled with, *call me now* and *it's an emergency.*

When I wasn't getting the information I wanted from the text messages, I decided to listen to the voice messages instead. The first voice message was from the friend who always had a sad story. I didn't even allow her to finish speaking. Just hit delete and moved on.

The next message was from Devon. He sounded frantic like something serious was going on. I hated hearing him this way. And knew I had to —

"You up baby?" Carson asked stretching and yawning.

"Oh yeah," I was about to set my phone down on the table so he couldn't see me scrolling but he was staring dead at me. For some odd reason he seems annoyed every time I had my phone. "Did you, um, did you sleep well? Because you were snoring hard."

"I slept like a baby. You really put me out last night."

"Are you serious? You're the one who constantly has to, what do you say, have some wet sugar." I laughed.

I had a feeling he was about to grab me and pull me into a hug. So, I stuffed my phone in the front of my panties. And just like I thought he pulled me closer. So that my body was lying next to his.

"So, what are your plans for today?" He asked.

"I was thinking about getting us some breakfast. I wanted to start there if it was cool with you."

"From Grannies?" He smiled.

"Is there any place else but Grannies? Because if it is, I can't call it."

He chuckled. "Cool, I'm gonna take a shower, clean up a little and wait for you to come back. That way we can eat and hit the streets."

The moment he gave me my out I quickly got dressed and moved toward the door grabbing my purse in the process. I was almost out when he said, "Hold up."

I turned to face him." What's up?"

"You didn't ask me what I wanted."

Big mistake. "I thought you wanted the usual." I shrugged. "Pancakes, bacon almost burned, eggs and sausage. Am I right?"

"You know me too well."

With my excuse in tow, I smiled and dipped out the door.

TAMMY

When I got to Devon's house, he was pulling himself out of his truck. I parked in someone's space, something I normally didn't do, to find out what was going on. "Devon, are you ok?"

He looked at me as if he wanted nothing to do with me. Plus, his face was banged up. Like he been in a fight and lost. He was also walking funny as if the perpetrator also punched him in the belly more than once. "What you want, Tammy? Or is it Carson?"

I shook my head. He knew damn well I wasn't Carson. "I couldn't answer the phone yesterday. I'm sorry about that. But I'm here now."

"Let me guess, your man didn't want you to?"

"I promise you it's not like that." I paused. "It's just that we were on a date and time got away from me. By the time I looked at my phone it was the morning. Are you okay though?" I got out of the car and followed him upstairs even though he didn't want me to.

"Go away."

He didn't mean it. So, when we made it in his apartment I asked, "Is everything okay with Miracle?"

He glared. "What do you want? Being here now it's not helping me. Just go back with your little boyfriend. It ain't like you give a fuck about your friends anymore since you got with the nigga."

"Devon, that's not fair."

"Get out, Tammy! I won't ask you again."

"Devon, please don't do this. I really am sorry but I—."

"If I ask you the fuck again, I'ma lay hands on you. Bounce! Now!"

I shook my head and turned around. As I walked out the door I thought about my life. It was as if I was playing tug of war with myself. The good part of me, the same as the rational part of me wanted to be with Carson. But my heart needed drama. My heart knew pain. It was as real as my skin. So how can you separate yourself from who you really are?

When I made it out of his building's door I ran into Jamie. She looked frazzled as if she had a lot on her mind. What was she doing there? I'm starting to believe

BY MERCEDES BISHOP

that my group of friends are cursed because we are always so stressed. Maybe we are involved in this weird nebulous relationship where we bring each down no matter what.

"What's up, Jamie?" I looked back at the door and then at her. "What are you doing here?"

"I'm so glad you're here. We have to talk. It's an emergency."

JAMIE

We were sitting at a diner looking at each other as if we were crazy. You have to understand Tammy and I used to be really close. In the beginning, outside of her spending most of her time with Devon, when she wasn't with him, she was always with me.

And then she betrayed me.

It wasn't anything drastic like you may think. It had more to do with her assumptions than anything else. Devon was having one of his parties and I made a mistake of bringing Brooklyn the wrong beer. He hurriedly pulled me back to Devon's room to talk to me in private.

So, what does Tammy sneaky ass do? She walked into the room and happened to see us fighting. We are married. People fight all the time. They put on like we were the only couple in the world that got physical.

So what, he slapped me. So what, she saw him. I needed to start treating him like the king he was, and I fucked up. Regardless of what people thought he was my husband and I had all intentions on making my marriage work.

"Why did you tell everybody that Brooklyn hit me that night?" I asked as we waited for our waitress to bring our meals. To tell you the truth I wasn't really hungry, but I wanted something to do with my hands.

She frowned. "Jamie, I walked in on him choking you. I, I was scared, and I guess, I guess I needed to tell someone."

"*We* were fighting!"

"He was hitting you and you were crying. That's not a fight."

"That's one version."

"I'm going to tell you something that you probably haven't heard but need to hear. When you're getting your ass beat that's not considered a fight. That's not considered an argument. You're getting abused."

"See this is the reason we can't be friends no more!" I pointed at her.

"Why?" She shrugged. "Because I don't stand by and watch you get hurt?"

"I can finally see that you're always gonna make it be whatever you want it to be. But just know that your behavior is the reason we aren't close anymore."

She sighed and clasped her hands in front of her. "Jamie, I know you didn't bring me here to talk about the past. So, tell me straight up what's going on? I mean, I know something's wrong. I can see it all over your face."

"Before I tell you this will you promise to keep it between me and you?" I whispered. "I need to hear the words."

"If I say yes, will you even believe me?"

Our waitress brought over our meals and neither one of us wanted to eat. We just stared at the plates trying to determine if we could trust each other let alone like each other. "Jamie, I love you. You know I do."

"I don't know that but it's whatever." I shrugged.

"I do, but I'm trying to get back over to Devon's. So, whatever you gotta tell me, make it count and make it quick."

"That's what I wanted to talk to you about." I looked down at my fingers which were trembling. I think she noticed because she reached over and touched my hand.

"Are you okay?"

I felt myself about to cry. "Brooklyn... I think he..."

"What is it?"

"I think he kidnapped Miracle."

DEVON

I was supposed to meet Penny fifteen minutes ago. I definitely wasn't doing myself any favors, but I had to build up the courage to say what needed to be said. At the end of the day, I fucked up on the money for Miracle. I mean, the plan started out simple. I was supposed to meet the kidnappers at a designated location. They also told me that I couldn't be followed. But what does my future father-in-law do?

Follows me anyway.

And these niggas, whoever they were, noticed and gave me clear instructions to get him lost. I did a good job of keeping him off my trail but once it was time to make the exchange, they felt like I wasn't being forthcoming, so they snatched the paper.

Fuck!

And now I had to meet this man and tell him I have no idea where his daughter is. I was so irritated like, I seriously thought about leaving town. I thought about moving to Texas or maybe even Alabama. I know some people think the southern states don't care for a nigga in the proper way, but I don't mind.

Down south, white folks got their rules and black folks got theirs. When we meet in the middle at restaurants every now and again its cool but most of the time we stay out of each other's way.

At the end of the day, I had to bounce. But not right now. Because contrary to what Penny believes I really want to find his daughter. And I'm a man before anything else.

After getting the money snatched, I stepped into the laundromat. The moment I closed the door I was punched in the stomach again and brought to my knees. Mind you his friends had done this shit earlier in the day. So why am I being hit again?

Penny walked up to me." Why did you lose me?"

I coughed a few times and rubbed my belly. "They saw you following me." I coughed a few more times. "And said, said if I didn't lose you, they would hurt Miracle."

"I don't believe you!"

"I wouldn't mess with your money, Penny! I swear to God!"

"You fucked with my money the moment you got with my daughter! Do you remember all the times I had to give you a little something on rent? Or...or when your car note was short? On your insurance? I'm starting to believe you think I'm the fucking bank!"

I stood on one knee. "If I think you're anything it's not the bank."

He glared and walked toward me. "Fuck is that supposed to mean?"

I stood up. "I didn't mean it that way! I'm just saying that I would never mess with your money. You're the one who gave me specific instructions on what the kidnappers said. Like I told your men, I guess they felt like you were going to call the police and got spooked. I don't know man." I shrugged. "All I know is they told me to lose you and that's what I did."

"Where is Miracle?"

"I don't know." I tossed one hand up. "I really wish I did."

He looked me over as if he was finally seeing me for the first time. I know this look. He had given it to me before Miracle and I first got together. I know he doesn't think I'm good enough for his daughter. To be honest, I think he's right. But in this instance, he's got me all wrong. I've done some cruddy shit in my lifetime but this ain't one of the times I fucked up.

"I feel in my heart that whoever is responsible is somebody the both of you know." He said.

I knew he was wrong. "I hear what you saying but everybody in my life has been around us for years. I got no new friends nowhere and can't think of one person who would do this to me."

"So, you're telling me that there is no new person who entered your life over the past few months?"

"I am because —."

"Before you answer I want you to think hard. Because this could be the difference between life and death."

I really wish I knew what this nigga wanted me to say so I could ice my ribs at home. At this point I'm like if you want to kill me then get it over with. But please don't blame me for something that I didn't do.

Besides, who the fuck would take money from Penny unless they stupid? Miracle doesn't even like taking money from him. This man is mean all the way through the core. And yet he thinks I will step to him about $100,000?

He obviously doesn't know me at all.

And then for some reason Tammy's new boyfriend entered my mind. Like, he seems like the kind of dude who could do this. I do find it fucked up that he doesn't want her anywhere around us. If I'm going to kidnap a friend, I would definitely separate my girl from the scenario.

Maybe it was him.

"Well? Do you know anybody or not?"

"Nah, man. I don't."

"You got less than 48 hours to find my daughter or bring my money back. Or it's your life."

CHAPTER, SOMETHING LIKE MADNESS

7

TAMMY

It was later in the afternoon, way past breakfast time, and I still wasn't home with Carson. After talking to Jamie and hearing what she said about Miracle's kidnapping, I had to see Devon. But this was a delicate situation. I had to try to find a way of telling him what I knew without revealing too much. Afterall, I made a promise.

Well...kinda.

I was driving down the street when my phone rang. The moment I saw Carson's number my stomach felt queasy and I sent the call to voicemail. I was supposed to be bringing breakfast. Instead, I was bringing him more irritation. I didn't want to lose him. That was true. I just wish he understood more about my relationship with my friends that's all. But he didn't.

When my phone rang again, I was hoping it was Devon, but it was even better. My mother. I quickly hooked my cord up to the car so it would play through my speakers. "Mama!" I said excitedly. "How are things in Korea?"

"It's business. And I'm safe and can't complain." She said. "How are you?"

"Fine. I mean…I guess I'm fine."

"Tammy…you don't sound too good."

I sighed. "It's Devon."

"There you go with that boy again."

"Mama, please."

"Listen, I know you hate when I preach, and God knows I try not to. But at the same time, you have to decide what you want right now."

"There's nothing to decide. I want Carson." I wish I said it with more authority, but it didn't come out that way.

"That's not what I mean." She sighed deeply. "Hold on, baby."

I could hear her walking and then I heard a door close, followed by a squeaky chair. I figured she must be in her office now. Seconds later she said, "Tammy, sorry about that. Are you there?"

"Yes, mama."

"Listen, sweetheart, when I first started using drugs it was to get over losing my mother. Losing her was the hardest thing I ever had to deal with and I…I didn't think I could survive without her. I wanted the pain to go away, so I reached for something to numb me. And that numbing drug was crack. And with that decision came so much more."

"You don't have to talk about it." I always got embarrassed when she talked about her drug use because those moments were dark in my life.

My mother may have been high ranking in the military, but before this point in her life, before I was born, she was an addict. To be honest I'm not sure how she was even selected in the military until she explained they don't care how you start, as long as you are clean, and nothing shows on the reports.

Personally, I think she didn't tell them.

"I want to talk about it, so you can understand." She sighed. "With that decision came a new host of problems and bad friends. And before long, it wasn't about my mother anymore. It was about the drama. The fight to get the drugs. The break ups with my just as addicted boyfriend. Tammy, I was in love with the madness. And I think you are too."

I pulled over and threw myself back in my seat. "It's not that. I just been knowing Devon for so long. He, he gets me in ways I can't explain."

"You did it again."

"What?"

"Connected my point with a person."

"Maybe I, I mean, maybe I don't understand. You mentioned your addicted boyfriends and—"

"Far as I know, Devon is not a boyfriend. Or did that change?"

She got me. "No, mama...we're just friends."

"Madness is a state of mind, Tammy. The cast and characters you attract while you're in this state is just the aftermath. If you want peace, those who refuse it won't even be near you. They wouldn't be able to deal with your energy. You will be on a higher scale."

When my phone beeped, I saw it was Devon and my heart pumped. "I gotta go, mama!" I hung up before she could dispute. "Devon, where are you?"

"Home. I need your help."

"I'm on my way."

TAMMY

BY MERCEDES BISHOP

When I pulled up to Devon's apartment building his car was double parked in front of the building. The passenger side door was open, and he was sitting sideways on the other side. I quickly parked my car and jumped out. Approaching him I asked, "Are you okay? You sounded really bad."

The moment I saw his battered and bruised face my heart sunk. It's one thing to beef with him but a whole different matter to stand by and watch him be hurt. While knowing I wasn't there when he needed me.

So, I closed my car door and parked his car. Then I parked mine in one of his two spots. Afterwards I helped him up the stairs. We didn't even talk about what happened at that moment. It didn't matter anyway. All that mattered was that he needed me and for some reason I needed him.

The first thing I did was put him on the sofa. He was moaning and I knew he was in deep pain. Then I gave him a frozen pack of peas which he placed on different parts of his body to cool the pain. I guess he was hurting everywhere. Next I prepared him a quick meal of spaghetti sauce noodles and garlic bread using slices. When everything was cooked, I fed him and gave him medicine for the pain.

While he was eating, I changed the linen on his bed ran his bath and helped him into the bathtub. He didn't want me seeing him naked, even though he needed my help washing up, so I stayed in his bedroom. If there was one thing, I knew it was how to take care of a person in pain.

When people suffered, something awoke in me and pulled me toward those who genuinely needed me. My mother thinks its madness. But maybe I want people to treat me the same way if I ever went through trials and struggles.

Because although my mother is doing well now, when she first had me, she would rip and run the streets. So, while I lived in foster homes, I had to do what was necessary to take care of me. And I wondered how I would be if I had someone like me around at that time.

After he was bathed, I helped him to bed. When he was tucked under the blankets, I took off my street clothes, grabbed one of his T-shirts and crawled in bed with him although I remained on top of the covers. We were facing one another.

I could feel his body relaxing and the tension melting away. "You don't have to stay." He said.

"I'm not leaving you." I touched his face with my palm. "How do you feel?"

"The truth?"

I smiled. He preferred to be difficult. "Ain't that what we do? Tell each other the truth?"

"Penny's giving me 48 hours to find his daughter. They kidnapped her."

This was worse than I thought. "Is that where you went today? To see Penny?"

He nodded yes. "He gave me the money and the niggas told me to come alone. But he followed and they saw him and took the money anyway. This nigga Penny blames me and then fucks me up in his laundromat." He sighed deeply. "I'm fucked up right now. For real, I don't even know what to do."

"Can I do anything?"

He looked at me for what felt like forever. "You already are."

We laid in silence for a few minutes. "Devon, I know you don't get me and Carson, but he isn't trying to take me away from my friends."

"Maybe not your friends."

"What does that mean?"

"Is he trying to take you away from *me*, Tammy? Because for real, that's all I care about."

Silence.

"I think he can help with your situation." I wanted badly to tell him what Jamie told me. But there were many reasons I decided against it. For starters, she already looked at me like I was disloyal. Telling him about something she wasn't sure about would set us back forever.

"How can he help?"

"He can ask around on the streets."

He frowned. "Get the fuck outta here with that shit. Nah."

"Do you have a choice?"

"I don't know about getting your folks mixed in."

"Time is running out, Devon. I mean if you got another plan, I'm open to it. Whatever you do I can't have you get hurt like this again. Just seeing you like…seeing you like this…" I felt myself on the verge of crying. "Never mind."

"I'm safe, Tammy."

"For now, Devon. You safe for now."

"Okay, if you think Carson can help. See what you can do."

I smiled and got out of bed.

TAMMY

When I made it to Carson's house, he was walking inside with grocery bags. The moment he saw my face he turned around and hit it for his door. "Get the fuck away from me, Tammy. I'm not playing around."

"Carson, I'm so sorry."

"Sorry for what this time? Saying you gonna bring breakfast and never showing back up? 'Cause if that's the case you always sorry."

"I know it may seem like I'm tripping but something really bad happened. This is not a game."

He opened his door and I tried to get in, but he placed his bags in the foyer, turned around and blocked my entry. "Listen, you a cute girl."

"A cute girl?" I frowned. "That's what you reduce me to now? Because the other night I was beautiful."

"Well it's the daytime now and I can see you clearly. Now what the fuck do you want? Because for real, we done."

We're done? Every time he said those words it cut deep but this time I felt like crying. And then for whatever reason I said, "Somebody kidnapped my cousin." I wept harder. So hard I started believing myself. "And I didn't want to tell you because I knew you wouldn't understand. "So many tears covered my eyes that suddenly I couldn't see. "And all you worried about is food when my family is scared! They're scared she may die!"

He stepped out. "Tammy, I—."

"But if you don't care I'll leave you alone." I turned to run to my car but before my foot hit the next step I was lifted up with a strong hold from behind. It was like I was floating.

He put his lips to my ear. "I'm so sorry, baby. I got you. Do you hear me?" His voice vibrated into my ear causing it to tickle.

I cried harder and, in that moment, embraced madness.

MIRACLE

Some man covered in a face mask brought me something to eat. At first, I didn't want to be bothered

BY MERCEDES BISHOP

but by this time I was so hungry I ate it all. And I hated to admit it, but it was good.

He was turning to leave when I said, "Wow, what, what is this?"

He stopped and faced me. "What's the problem?"

"Nothing. It's good. And to be honest I wasn't expecting it that's all."

He folded his arms and unfolded his arms. I couldn't see his face, but I could tell he was smiling. "Well, thank you. I don't get a lot of compliments around here so that means a lot. Thank...thank you."

"Well you need to get more compliments. Because if you cooked this you put your foot into the meal."

He nodded repeatedly, almost like a bobble head. "Thank you. That made my—."

A knock at the door sent him running upstairs. In his rush, he closed the door but forgot to lock it. My heart thumped because I had been praying nonstop for a way out of it all. Was this God's way of answering my prayers? If I refused to heed the call would I get another break?

Feeling dizzy, I pushed my plate to the side and jumped up. Opening the door slowly I ascended the first step and the voice I heard next rocked my soul. It hurt me in a way I didn't know possible.

Why would he do this to me?

He was my friend.

The voice I heard was Brooklyn's.

TAMMY

I was sitting in his living room on the sofa, desperately trying to inhale the scent of the vanilla plug in's Carson had throughout his house, to rest my nerves. It wasn't working. Although I liked them in the past, as of now it was making me nauseous.

While he was on the phone, calling every person he knew to tell them that his girlfriend's cousin, Miracle, had been kidnapped I felt dizzy. In less than twenty minutes he flooded the streets that he would pay big money for information.

When he was done, he made me a tall glass of wine and sat next to me. This man was good. He looked legit concerned about my lying ass and the cousin who was really a friend. And because of it at the moment I couldn't stand my guts.

"Thank you. For, for everything, Carson."

BY MERCEDES BISHOP

"Bae, I'm sorry I treated you so badly. You needed me and I knocked you down without letting you speak."

I was about to cry again because the lie was so strong it was in full flex. "It's fine, Carson. You're here for me now and that's all that matters."

"Nah. You needed me and I...damn..." he stood up.

I sniffled. "Carson, I don't blame you for any of this. And I appreciate whatever you can do to help me. Seriously."

He walked back toward me. "I'm gonna find out who got her." He said with force. "I promise you that."

CHAPTER, IT'S ONLY HER

8

JAMIE

This car was a complete mess. It was like a puzzle and doing the wrong thing would cause it to shut down. So, I was driving down the street trying not to push the gas too hard. Not to hit the brakes too hard. Trying not to turn the wheel too hard. At the end of the day this car stressed me out.

After stopping by the neighborhood to get me a 20 bag of weed I was going to the fast food to get some steak and cheese sandwiches. At the same time, I was wondering what was going on with Tammy. We talked about a lot the last time I saw her. Starting with trying to come up with a plan to help Miracle without letting on that Brooklyn was involved. I didn't feel comfortable with any scenario and pretty much said that maybe I had gotten it wrong. That maybe Brooklyn didn't say what I thought I heard.

At this point I just needed to make sure she wasn't freaking out, which would bring me more drama. So far, every time I reached out to her, she seemed to ignore my

BY MERCEDES BISHOP

calls. My only hope was that she would keep my secret and not tell Devon. But it's not like she hadn't told my secrets before.

After grabbing the sandwiches, I parked the car and it immediately cut off. Literally, the moment I pulled into my parking space the car cut off. My heart rate jumped because I had so much to do over the course of the week. I had to grocery shop. I had to go to work. I had to pick up Brooklyn's clothes from the cleaners. But I could do nothing without transportation. Brooklyn would not want to hear that my car was not working even though it wasn't my fault. So, I stood in the parking lot giving it time to cool off. When 15 minutes past I tried to start the car. Again, it wouldn't turn over.

This is not good. I immediately broke down crying. This would set me and Brooklyn back another two weeks, I'm sure. He did not do well with drama. His answer for everything wrong was always that it was my fault. In most cases it was my fault. But in all cases I tried to make things better before bringing the issue to him. But he never wanted to hear what I tried to do. He only wanted the problem to go away.

After realizing my car was officially broke, I tried to think of things I could do to make my life easier before telling him. The first thing I did was roll a blunt. It wasn't as thick as I like, but it would have to do right now.

Then I ate a sandwich right there in the car. It was messy, cheesy, greasy and so much more. And for some reason it calmed me. Yes, it was more calories than Brooklyn allowed. But my plan was to walk 20,000 steps and pay for this meal. Not really sure if walking really helps but it makes me feel better. Mainly because it's a self-imposed punishment. Which I deserve.

When I was done, I went upstairs and prepared for the worst by fixing what I could. The house was clean, so I didn't have to bother with that too much. And then I thawed out some chicken which I knew we ate the day before yesterday, but my plan was to chop it up fine and put it in a casserole so he wouldn't detect it.

Right before getting started with the meal, Brooklyn came home. I did all I could to hold my bladder. As usual I studied his face closely. Trying to check his mood to see what kind of day it would be. "Hey…hey."

"Hey, bae." He smiled.

That's a good sign! A, a, smile means he's not angry. It means, it means I'll have a good day. If I did the right thing, if I said the right thing, I can ease into telling him about the car slowly. And then maybe he won't take it as bad. Maybe he won't hit me.

Maybe, maybe he —."

"Bae," he frowned. "Why you looking all crazy? You good over there?"

I wanted to hug him because he was in a happy mood but suddenly all I could do was cry. "No, no I'm not."

He rushed up to me, "What's wrong?"

"Nothing, I'm, I'm sorry…"

He held me. "Sorry for what?"

"The car, the car broke down and, and I know you want me to handle things before I come to you but I…I mean…I…"

He held me tighter.

Why was he holding me tighter? With the exception of the earlier part of our relationship, I never knew Brooklyn to embrace me when I was like this. It irritated him mostly and so I would cry alone, in the bathroom. So why was he holding me so lovingly now?

"Jamie, stop crying." He laughed. "You tripping like shit over here."

I was trying. "I'm…I'm…I'm…I'm sorry."

"Stop being sorry." He paused. "Everything's gonna be good."

He was smiling harder and everything felt stupid, weird and nice at the same time. I nodded my head up and down and took a deep breath. "Okay."

"Come with me." He grabbed my hand and before I knew it, we were standing outside of our building.

Parked in an available space to the right was a new white Hyundai. It had paper tags and everything. "Brooklyn...what...what is this?" I wiped the tears away.

"It's yours."

I placed both of my hands on the side of my face. "Are you, are you serious?"

"I wouldn't play like this. You needed a car and I wanted you to have one. And judging by what you said, it couldn't come at a better time."

"But...but how? How were we able to do this?"

He glared. "I give you a gift and you ask how?"

I felt a weight in the pit of my stomach. There I go again fucking shit up. "No, I mean, thank you."

He smiled again, reached in his pocket and dropped the keys in my hand. "Take it for a spin. Like I said, it's a gift."

I held the keys in my hand like a precious diamond and hugged him tightly. "Thank you, Brooklyn! Thank you!" I looked back at my bucket. I would never have to deal with that car again.

My emotions were so all over the place. One moment I felt like he was minutes from beating me and the next he gives me an unbelievable gift. "What you want me to do with my car?"

"I'll take care of..." his phone rang, and he looked down at it. "Listen, take it for a drive and meet me back at the house later." He focused back on the phone although he didn't move.

I didn't move either.

"Fuck you still doing here?" He paused. "Go!"

I ran off.

JAMIE

I had been everywhere in my car.

My mama's house. My cousin Jenkins apartment who always bragged about what her boyfriend gave her and even my sister's job. Everybody liked my car and seemed shocked that Brooklyn would do something so nice for me. I knew why they were surprised. They thought he was too jealous and too mean to do anything for me. Without knowing my part in why he was frustrated all the time.

After doing a tour, I was just about to go home when Tammy called. "Hey, girl," I said excitedly.

"Jamie…" She paused for a minute. "Are you…are you okay?"

I frowned. Just that quickly I forgot about what I told her. "Yeah, why you say that?"

"For starters you're a little too happy considering our friend has been kidnapped."

And as if something hit me over the top of my head, I knew where Brooklyn got the money. Suddenly I pushed the door open and vomited on the side of the road. When I was done, I sat back in the car.

"Hello!" I heard her yell.

"Yes."

"Jamie, what's going on? Were you just throwing up?"

I wiped my mouth with the back of my hand. "Yeah, what do you want?"

"You been calling me nonstop and now that I hit you up you don't have no convo for me?"

"I was busy."

"Okay, so what we gonna do with the Miracle situation? And Brooklyn?"

"We?"

"Yes, you said you thought Brooklyn—."

"I don't know what you talking about."

"Jamie, you, you said you—."

"I said I don't know what you talking about. And if you try to lie on me, I'll deny everything. Now leave me alone!" I hung up before she could respond, threw up again and cried in my brand-new ride.

DEVON

I went to get something to eat, although my face and body still hurt after fucking with Penny. On my way home I decided to hit Tammy to see if she was able to come up with anything from her dude. To be honest I wasn't feeling much like hitting her up about him, but I needed help.

"Hey, how you feeling?" I asked when she picked up.

"I'm more concerned about you." Her voice was soft and soothing.

I looked in my rearview mirror and saw the same black Honda I saw earlier. "I'm concerned about me too."

"I'm sorry you gotta go through this shit, Devon. Like for real."

"Don't worry about it. No matter what, I gotta deal you know?" I sighed. "Was your mans able to find out anything?"

"He hasn't told me anything yet. He's —."

I knew this nigga was a fluke. "Don't worry about it, Tammy."

"Wait, what?"

"I been feeling like asking you was a weird flex since you said he would help. I mean, it ain't like I fuck with the dude."

"Devon, don't be like that."

"Don't be like what?" I shrugged. "Not wanting your man to come to my rescue? Like I'm some kind of bitch?"

"He wants to help."

"That's the thing I don't get." I looked out the rearview mirror and the black Honda was still following me. "Why did he agree to help?"

"Because you're like a brother to me."

I sighed. "Oh yeah?"

"Why you say that?"

"I don't know…just can't see you and I as siblings."

"You know what I'm saying. You should start trusting people more."

"Ain't about trust. Just makes no since that the one nigga who been trying to keep me away from you suddenly gonna come to the rescue."

"I know what I know. And this man cares for me. He will help."

"That's nice for you."

"Devon, I'll hit you back."

I hung up without another word.

I'm sick of going back and forth with her about dude. Instead, I was going to hit it back home when I thought about Brooklyn. I give him a hard time, but he's a real one. When I first started my business, I asked all of my friends to go into it with me. The first person I went to was Tammy, and she flat out said no. I never got a good reason why she wasn't interested, but I had a feeling she didn't believe in me. That was cool. She was entitled. But Brooklyn never wavered.

When I parked alongside his apartment building, I saw Brooklyn yelling at a nigga. On top of a car they were standing by, was a plate wrapped in aluminum foil. Brooklyn's arms were waving high and it looked like he was about to hit dude.

Fuck was going on?

After what seemed like too long, dude tried to hand Brooklyn the plate, but he knocked it out of his hand, and it hit the ground.

"Fuck you do that shit for?" The dude asked.

"Cause I'm not here for all that!" Brooklyn responded.

"You know what, fuck you too!" The man yelled before getting into the car and pulling off.

Before Brooklyn reached his building, I parked and stepped to him. "Aye, aye, Brooklyn!"

He turned around and looked like he saw a ghost. "Oh...oh hey, man." He scratched the top of his head.

"Who was that nigga?" I asked, pointing in the direction he left with my thumb.

He stopped and tucked his hands in his pocket. "Nobody. What you, what you doing out here?"

"So, you yell at nobody that hard?"

He frowned. "You...you heard what we were saying?" He crossed his arms over his chest.

"Nah, but I saw how you were acting. Are you cool?"

He released his arms. "It ain't about nothing for real."

For some reason Brooklyn being gay entered my mind. "Listen, man, if you go that way I ain't gonna judge you. My aunt's nephew a little sweet around the—."

"I'm not gay," he said cutting me off.

I nodded. "Okay, okay, well something ain't adding up."

"Look, man, it's been a long day. All I wanna do is take a shower, get in bed and grab a nap."

Just then Jamie pulled up in a brand-new car. I frowned. "Hold up, she got a new job?"

Jamie exited her car, looked at me and dipped into the building. All without saying hello. That was unlike her because when we were all together, she looked at me like I was a savior sometimes.

"Is Jamie good?" I asked. "She looked rattled."

"Damn, my nigga. Any other time I can't get conversation and now you asking a million questions."

I glared. "Fuck that mean?"

"It means I'm busy and I'ma hit you later." He dapped my hand. "Okay?"

I nodded and he walked away.

What the fuck was that? And why didn't he ask about Miracle?

CHAPTER, ENEMIES BE MY FRIENDS

9

TAMMY

I was sitting at Carson's house on the living room sofa while he argued with a lady who didn't like the renovations in her home. He didn't say his mood change was because of me, but I got the impression that he wasn't focused on his job because of my situation and so his work suffered.

When he ended the call, he walked over to his bar. "You drinking?" He poured himself a glass of Hennessey.

"Is everything good?" I asked in a soft voice.

He turned around. "You want something or nah?"

I swallowed. "Uh, yeah, I'll take some wine."

He made our drinks and sat next to me. Drinking half of the glass down he said, "We forgot to connect her toilet to the plumbing. And she mad cause shit fell on the floor and...it's crazy."

I squinted my nose. "Eww, so what was wrong. I mean how bad is—."

"Everything splashed around." He took another sip. "I got somebody going over there now but of course she trying to claim damage."

I sat my glass down. "Carson—."

"Drink your wine."

I sipped lightly and sat it down on the floor. "Carson, if my situation fucking with your money, I'm sorry."

He glared. "This has nothing to do with you."

"I hear you, but you never make mistakes. We joke all the time about how you're a perfectionist. Something ain't adding up."

He drank the rest of his liquor and pulled me closer to him. Kissing the top of my head he said, "I won't lie, the situation with your cousin has been on my mind. But that's what happens when you care about somebody."

But what happens when someone lies? I thought.

"But this is your livelihood." I continued.

"And I'll be fine." He pulled me even closer and I could feel the heat from his body. "We gonna find who grabbed shawty and—."

KNOCK. KNOCK. KNOCK.

He pushed me lightly and I moved so he could get up and answer the door. Within seconds his cousin

Brian and two other guys came inside. They looked all business and I immediately felt uncomfortable.

"This my girl, Tammy," Carson said pointing at me. "You would've met her if you came to the party she threw for us."

"Yeah," Brian said.

I didn't move. I couldn't move. Why were they there?

They all nodded at me and walked inside and found places to sit. Brian sat next to me and for some reason I could feel the heat off his body too. Like he kinda, maybe, didn't like me.

"Ya'll drinking?" Carson asked.

Brian looked at me and back at him. "Nah, we good." He sighed. "So, tell me what's going on again."

My heart was beating fast. Why was my heart beating fast? And then I heard the words that made me feel faint.

"Tell him what you told me, babe." Carson said. "About your people. We gonna get down to the bottom of this shit tonight."

"My cousin, she was, kidnapped."

Brian frowned. "He told me that. Need more."

I shifted. "She, I mean, she wasn't, I mean actually she didn't..." For some reason I broke out into a nervous laughter and everyone, but Carson, glared.

"You seem a little off." Brian said. "What's wrong?"

"Off?"

"Yeah, like you lying."

My jaw dropped. "What...why...who...I mean...I'm definitely not lying."

He stared at me for a while. I meant to keep his gaze, but I got scared and looked away. The moment I did he said, "She lying, cuz." He stood up. "I don't trust this chick at all."

His men rose too.

"Fuck you talking about?" Carson said.

Brian tapped Carson's shoulder and they walked to the back. His two friends maintained their stares at me. If they hadn't been there I would've took to the streets I was so scared. Scared I was caught in my lie. Scared he would convince Carson. And scared I would lose him for good.

While they were in the back, I didn't make out much conversation. I heard the words, *name*, *disrespect*, and *liar*. But that was it. Fifteen minutes later Carson came out and opened the door, Brian was close behind.

When they were gone and we were alone, I asked, "Is everything okay?"

"We have to find another way." He walked in the back. "Fuck his ass."

I smiled knowing he chose me.

MIRACLE

I found out something odd today.

When you're kidnapped, after a while, people forget you are there. You become like an old piece of furniture, unworthy of care or attention. They talk about you and even around you, never really caring if you hear them or not. And that's what was happening to me now. But was their attitude around me indicative of me going to die?

Is that why me hearing didn't matter?

At the same time, being a wallflower was a blessing. My daddy said the world throws gifts to those who are aware. When you sit in the silence, when you listen more and talk less, you learn everything. And after everything I heard upstairs, I felt smarter now.

When the front door slammed closed, my door opened and the ski mask man came inside, holding a plate. Before I even got it, the smell was pleasing.

"I made something special for you to try." He handed me the plate. On top of it was a napkin and a knife and fork. Next he did something he normally didn't do, sat on the floor next to the door. "Tell me what you think."

I removed the aluminum foil and took a bite. It was spaghetti doused with a cheese sauce and garlic bread. "Oh my...oh my god." It really was amazing. Whoever this man was he could cook.

His cheeks rose in his ski mask. "Stop playing."

"No, I promise you this, this is really good."

He moved around. "You don't think it's too much garlic?"

"Fuck no."

I saw his cheeks rise again. "I was worried I did too much."

"If you changed this recipe, I would hurt you."

He laughed. "You don't know how good that makes me feel."

"I'm just being honest. You must have women fighting over your food."

He looked down. "Nah, I don't."

BY MERCEDES BISHOP

"You single?" I said flirtatiously. As if my pussy and underarms didn't funk up the spot.

"Stop it."

"What?" I shrugged. "Just because you kidnapped me doesn't mean we can't be cordial. Right?"

He nodded. "I'm single."

"Well cooking like this you won't be for long."

When I looked down at the plate a little closer, I saw a dead fly. Immediately my stomach churned, and I wanted to toss the plate across the room. But after wondering how many more bugs I already ate, I pushed it to the side and took another bite. "So, do you know how long, I'll...you know...be here?"

"Let's not talk about that."

"What? My freedom?"

"Yes."

I sighed and put the plate down. "I think you should know something. And I don't want you to get mad."

"Okay...what is it?"

"Brooklyn talked to me. Came down here one night."

He stood up and hung by the door. "You lying."

"I'm not." I paused. "He wanted me to ask my father for more money and then the plan was to set you up. To pretend like you kidnapped me and he saved me. He's not your friend."

"You better be careful with me. I don't fuck with liars."

"I'm being honest." I said in a low voice. "I like you more than I like him. Which is why I'm telling you now."

He stared at me hard. Dark eyes penetrating my soul. I now wondered if I'd made a mistake. It's not like I haven't fucked up in the past. Before I could get my bearings together, he walked over to me, kicked me in the side and walked out the door, slamming it behind himself.

There I was, lying on my side, in the dark crying softly. I never came to terms with what it meant to die. There wasn't a lot I appreciated in life to tell you the truth. I didn't appreciate my father's hugs even when he was being mean. I didn't appreciate my clients who gave me tips when I did their lashes. I didn't appreciate the sun coming up every day, despite the terrible things I may have done on earth. I didn't appreciate the moon shining bright at night, because I stayed inside away from the stars. I didn't appreciate my body working. My heart beating and my mind operating for me every day.

If I was given another chance, just one, I would be grateful.

Thankful.

Everyday.

An hour later, when the pain ripped through my body even more, the door opened again. And Mr. Ski Mask stepped inside and said, "How much money you think you can get from your father if I let you go?"

I smiled. "A lot."

DEVON

Penny said he'd be in the house in an hour and my nerves were wrecked. I thought about the position I was in and borrowed a gun from one of my cousins. There was no way I was going to allow him to kill me. If I was going out, I was going out swinging and I was taking him, or one of his men with me.

A lot was on my mind at the moment. Miracle. Tammy. And then, what was that thing with Brooklyn? What was that weird situation where he was yelling at a man and dropping plates on the ground like they were in a relationship? It made me uneasy but I didn't know why.

When there was a knock at my door, I opened it quickly, ready for whatever. The moment I saw Tammy's face, I smiled. Why did I smile?

"Aye, what's up?" I said opening the door wider.

"Why do you have that gun?"

I forgot it was in my hand. "No reason." I tucked it in my waist.

She locked the door and walked inside, flopping on the sofa. "You look rattled. You want me to leave?"

I shrugged. "Why you say that?"

"Because you look like you mad."

I sat next to her. "Penny's coming over."

"Is that why you got the gun?"

I nodded yes.

Her eyes widened and she placed a hand on my thigh. "Are you okay?"

I looked at her hand and then her eyes. "Yeah."

She removed her hand. "I'm sorry."

"For what?"

"Always touching you."

"Tammy, we go back. Don't be that way with me."

"So, what you gonna do? About Penny?"

"I'm not letting him fuck with me."

"Meaning?"

"Just what I said. He already disrespected. Beat me down. Had me followed. I mean, I had the man's money taken without finding his daughter. I understand the frustration. But I will defend myself. What you expect me to do?"

"You haven't said anything yet, Devon. What is your plan?"

I was silent. Not knowing if I could trust her enough to let her know I was gonna kill Penny. "I don't trust Brooklyn." When I said the words, it fucked me up. It wasn't what I planned to say.

Her eyes widened and she stood up. "Why...why you say that?"

I frowned. "Why you stand up?"

She looked on the floor, as if searching for something. When we were kids, she did this all the time when she knew a secret but was sworn to protect it.

I got up and walked toward her. "What is it?"

"Nothing."

I grabbed her shoulders and for some reason she moved to the floor, standing on her knees. I went down with her. "Tammy, talk to me."

She looked at me. "Brooklyn."

I frowned. "What about him?"

"I…I can't."

"Tammy, fucking talk to me before I unleash."

"I promised." She shook her head softly from left to right.

"And you gonna keep that promise? Over me? Over everything we represent. Over everything we've been through?"

"I, I don't have a choice."

"But why?"

I took a deep breath. Based on how she was acting, I felt she needed help. Like a nudge almost. "Tammy, I saw Brooklyn talking to this nigga outside his crib. It didn't feel good. Is what you want to tell me related?"

She nodded. "Yes. Jamie told me she overheard him mentioning Miracle's name to a guy when she eavesdropped on him at the house. She said it didn't sound right. But she isn't sure if he was involved with anything. Just that it felt weird."

I stood up and helped her up too. "I gotta make a run."

"Where to?"

"Brooklyn's."

CHAPTER, WE KNOW WHAT WE KNOW

10

BROOKLYN

The rain was a monster tonight. It had been nonstop, and I wanted it to let up. But the world didn't care what I wanted.

I was standing in the mirror, looking at this gold chain with diamonds piece I copped from the jewelers. The plan was to take my wife out to a nice spot later tonight for dinner. Feeling the occasion, she wanted to look pretty. So, she was at her cousin's crib, getting her hair braided up or some shit like that.

With the money I copped from Miracle's father, I made out okay. But it wasn't enough paper for my plans. After discussing it with Berkley, we looked at the first 100k as a down payment since Penny broke the rules by following Devon. With the next drop, after splitting it with Berks, I was planning to move out of town for good. And then, we'd kill Miracle.

Berkley was angry that he didn't get his cut yet, but I needed to wait it out to see if I could trust him. At the same time, I gave him a few bucks to make good on child support, but he wanted the entire fifty g's.

I said nah. Not yet.

He said it would come back to bite me later.

I told him to suck my dick.

When someone knocked at the door I frowned. Jamie had a thing with losing her key which made me wanna fuck her up. But I didn't want to spoil the mood. Taking a deep breath, I opened the door and was immediately shocked to see Devon with his cousin Viking.

"What up, man? I was just about to—."

Devon pushed inside before I could finish my sentence. They sat on the sofa and looked up at me. Something was up. "Where you going? You looking pretty shiny."

"On a date with my wife." I pointed at the door with my thumb.

"Is she here?" Devon frowned. "I wanted to rap to her too. Since she ain't have no words for me earlier."

"Nah. She...she getting her hair done." They know. They fucking know. But how?

"So, we'll wait until she get here." Devon said. "That is, if you don't mind."

"Everything cool?"

"I don't know." Viking said. "Is it?"

My heart thumped and although I wasn't sure, I swore I saw a hump on Devon's hip. Did he know? If he did, how? "Ya'll wanna play Madden until she gets here?" I asked.

"Nah, ain't in the mood for games. But I'm hungry," Viking said.

That was different. Most niggas asked for a beer. He wanted a plate. What type of shit is this? "What you want?" I asked scratching my head.

"What you got?"

"Hot dogs with—."

I'll take it."

I went in the kitchen and slammed a pot on the stove with water, while looking out the corner of my eye the entire time. Whenever I got a glimpse, they were staring at me.

"Ya'll sure you don't want a drink?" I asked, plopping the hot dogs in the pot. The water splashed in my face.

"Nah." Devon said.

"I do." Viking said. "What you got?"

"Can you stop being so fucking greedy?" Devon said to him through clenched teeth.

I rolled my eyes. That big nigga was getting on my nerves. But I didn't like the feel of this shit, so I had to play along. "Wanna beer?"

He nodded yes.

After serving him the drink, I sat on the recliner. "So, what you been up to today?"

Devon shrugged. "Not much. Still trying to find my girl."

"You...you...you...you..." I paused. "I mean...you — ."

"Are you aight?" Viking asked. "What's up with the stuttering?"

"Ain't nothing up."

"You acting like something on your heart." Viking said.

"Listen, I don't know what's up but I ain't stuttering. Ain't got no reason to. All I wanted was to spend some time with my wife. And the next thing I know ya'll over here moving different."

There was a knock at the door, and I was relieved. When I opened it my next-door neighbor's kid was on the other side. Normally I slammed the door in the little nigga's face, because he was always begging but my wife liked him. Today, at this moment, I liked him too.

"What's up, kid?" I smiled at him, before looking back at Devon and Viking who were both looking my way.

"Why you smiling and shit? You 'on't even like me."

"Lil nigga, what you want?" I looked back at Devon and Viking who were still looking our way, before focusing back on the kid.

"You got some pizza?"

I frowned. "Pizza?"

"Yeah, I'm hungry. I know you got your groceries."

"Where your mother at?"

"She not here." He shrugged. "That's why I'm asking you."

"He can have my hot dog," Viking said. "As long as he gets the fuck."

I quickly ran to make his food and handed it back to him. When we were alone again, I felt it was time to see what the deal was.

"The beer." Viking said.

"What?"

"Before the kid came you were gonna give me a beer."

I nodded. "I gave it to you. You sat it on the floor."

"Oh."

I finally realized he didn't want the hot dog or beer. He was trying to feel me out. "So, what's this visit about? Because I got the feeling—."

KNOCK. KNOCK. KNOCK.

Figuring the kid was back, I yanked the door open. Who I saw on the other end stumped me. It was Miracle.

As if he saw a ghost, Devon rose and rushed over to the door. Grabbing her up he said, "Bae, where the fuck have you been? Where the fuck were you?"

Her voice was low, and I couldn't hear what was being said. My heart was thumping so loudly, it blocked out sound. Not only was she supposed to be under the house, she wasn't supposed to be here.

"I'm sorry, I was kidnapped and finally fought my way out!" She kissed him and kissed him again. "It was the most horrifying time of my life."

Although she was talking to him, she was looking at me. Suddenly I felt sick. Why did I get rid of my gun? These niggas were no doubt going to kill me after finding out I was involved.

"What you doing here though?" Devon asked. "Why you ain't go to the house?"

Time seemed to slow. Was she about to say I was involved and if she was, what would happen to me next?"

BY MERCEDES BISHOP

"You weren't home," she said. "And I knew you'd be over here." She kissed him again. "But I'm home now! And I'm about to put everything back right."

TAMMY

Me and Carson were about to watch Netflix in the living room, when he looked over at me. His stare seemed intense and I felt a serious conversation coming. "Do you really wanna leave?"

I frowned. "I thought we were about to watch TV."

"No, I mean to Atlanta."

"Yeah, of course I wanna go." I nodded so much my head hurt.

He nodded. "I'm putting a lot on the line with you. You get that don't you?"

"I know, Carson." I sat on the sofa and grabbed a pillow, putting it in the middle of my lap.

"And I've been so fucked up about this shit lately. With your people."

"Is it because of Brian?"

He frowned. "Why you say that?"

"Because I know he doesn't like me. Or believe me."

"I wouldn't say that. He doesn't trust you though."

"But what could I be lying about?" *Everything bitch.*

"You know how my friends are. I told you that from the gate. They are overprotective when—."

"I guess, that's what I have a problem with. You talk about me and my friends being so clingy, but your friends are worse."

"What you mean?"

"You try to keep me from Devon and—."

"I find it interesting how you always bring up that man."

"If you're saying there's anything going on between me and him, you're wrong. What I'm trying to say is—."

"Nah, what *I'm* trying to say is that you play games. And I think you're leading me on. I think all of this, is to see how far I will go, Tammy."

My chest fell up and down. "Where is this coming from, Carson? You say it isn't about your friends or cousin but I'm starting to think other shit now."

When my phone rang, I ran to the end table. Normally I wouldn't pick it up, but I was tired of hearing him talk. If he wanted to accuse me of shit, then so be it. When I looked down, I saw it was Devon. I quickly answered mostly out of spite. "Hey, are you okay?"

When I looked over at Carson, he rolled his eyes and walked to the sink. "Tell your boy Devon I said hi."

I rolled my eyes and focused back on the call.

"Miracle is here." He whispered.

My eyes widened. "What? How?"

"I was over Brooklyn's preparing to step to him about what we talked about and she walked in."

"Why did she go there first?"

"Said she was looking for me."

"Oh my God, this is so good!" I said excitedly. "Did she mention anything about where she was?"

"No, but its freaking me the fuck out." He paused and started talking to someone in the background. "I'ma hit you back."

The call ended.

I looked at Carson, eager to share the happy news. "Carson, my friend is back home!"

He turned toward me. "Miracle?"

"Yeah! She popped up over Brooklyn's out of nowhere."

He frowned. "So, the chick you had me thinking was missing was actually your friend? And not your cousin?"

The moment he repeated what I said I knew I fucked up. This is why I hated lying. Could never keep up with it. "Yeah, uh, she's like a cousin to me. I —."

"Get out."

"Carson, I'm sorry. I just —."

"Get the fuck out before I lay hands on you! I'm not telling you again!"

TAMMY

I was in a hotel room.

Don't ask me why I didn't go home because I don't know. If I thought about it a lot, I would probably say because even though my house was in my name, it was still Carson's property. And even though I paid him every month, he gave the rent money back each time.

After taking a bath, I scrolled on the internet for a little while. At this point I was just trying to clear my mind. Trying to find something to do to make sense of my messy life. I know some people would look at me and say this was all my fault. The fact that I had a good boyfriend and lost him and the fact that I told a little

BY MERCEDES BISHOP

white lie. But my world was crashing down around me. And I genuinely wanted to help Devon. And I genuinely wanted to be with Carson.

After lying in bed and looking at a boring television show I got a call from Devon. I quickly sat up. "Hello?" My breath was heavy.

"What you doing?"

"What am I doing? What you doing? I just knew you would be celebrating Miracle being home."

"Nah." He sighed. "The moment we came back home her father came over and scooped her up. I don't know what they're doing now. All I really know is they don't seem to want me around."

"You want to come over here? I rented a hotel room. We can order takeout and chill."

"Where you get money from?"

"The truth?"

"You know I like the truth."

"Carson gave me a check. It cleared earlier today. I was supposed to be using it to find my new business. But now all I wanna do is — ."

"Give me the address."

After giving him the address, I got cleaned up and waited for him anxiously. We may have been just friends but when I was with Devon everything seemed to work out. Everything seemed to click in place, like a puzzle piece.

The moment he came over we got in bed. Clothes on as usual. The television was on but neither one of us was watching. I knew then that at sometime and at some point, in our lives we had become each other's comfort zone. When things were going bad, he needed to see me. And when things were going bad, I needed to see him. Maybe that's why we disgust everybody around us.

"Are you and Carson really over this time?"

I sighed. "I...I think so."

"Good."

I smiled and my stomached flipped a little. "Why you say that?"

"No reason." He shrugged.

"If we do anything in this world, we need to always tell each other the truth. The way things are going on in my life even if it's my problem or my fault I need things to stay the same with you, Devon. Honesty please."

He took a deep breath. "Okay, well, I say good because with him out the picture maybe we can get back to normal. Whatever that means."

I smiled again. "I believe you. And I'm so glad you're here."

CHAPTER, PAY FOR YOUR BETRAYAL

11

MIRACLE

I was waiting in the parking lot of a bowling alley. Waiting to meet Berkeley. If I explained my story to anyone else, they'd think I was crazy. But there was a method to my thought process. Yes, along with Brooklyn, he helped kidnap me. But I saw things differently. Besides, I would turn this situation in my favor.

"Wow, you actually came," he said easing into my car.

"An agreement is an agreement."

"You could've broken it though. And not paid me. And there wouldn't be anything I could do."

"Well you could have kept me in the basement, but you didn't." And then something dawned on me. "Why *did* you let me go?"

"You gonna think I'm crazy but, I let you go because, well, you liked my food."

"So, you let me out because I liked your food? Are you serious?"

"This kidnapping shit was never me. I didn't want to do none of it. All I wanted was to start a business and take care of my kids. But it's tough getting a job when you got a record. So, either I'm going to make the most out of this cooking thing or I'm done."

When I looked into his eyes the same eyes that were partially covered with the ski mask the day before, I could tell he was telling the truth. It didn't give him a right to do what he did. And at the same time, he was no more guilty than Brooklyn.

"I got you. But do me a favor and don't say anything to Brooklyn. I'm going to get the money from him and then I'll pay you."

"He's been hitting my phone nonstop."

"Saying what?"

"He wants to know why you out. He sent a couple of threats my way but for the most part it's all hype. I don't scare easily."

"Well what did he want to happen?"

"The truth?"

"You have my money. The least you could do is keep it 100 with me."

"He wanted me to kill you. He didn't say it originally because the plan was to hit Penny for another hundred grand. But I think he was hoping I'd make the situation go away by myself. And then he would run off with all the money."

When he said those words, a chill ran through my body. I always felt like I wasn't supposed to make it out of that house alive. And at the same time whenever I prayed my prayer was answered. But now after hearing him, I definitely believe Brooklyn deserves any ill will coming his way. But I would deal with him in the future.

"Let me go get your money." I said.

At the moment I heard enough from Berkeley and decided to go to my next appointment. I pulled up in the parking lot of a hole in the wall bar. Parked next to the car of the person I was meeting and walked inside.

Once inside I had to squint to look through the bar. It was dark and many other faces were concealed as if trying to hide from other people and themselves. It didn't take me long to spot Brooklyn. The whites of his eyes were turned toward me, and he looked nervous.

I sat next to him. Extra close. I wanted him to know I wasn't afraid. My focus was geared to the bartender. "What you drinking?" He asked.

I gave the bartender my order. Hennessey on the rocks. The moment he left I smiled at Brooklyn. "I guess you didn't expect to see me? Did you?"

His forehead was moist. "What you going to do?"

I shrugged. "I don't know. What do you think I should do to the man who tried to have me kidnapped and *killed*?"

"Tried to have you kidnapped? If I'm not mistaken, I succeeded."

"So, you think this funny?" I glared.

"No! I...listen this isn't what it seems to be. I was never going to hurt you. I only wanted—."

Lies.

"Money. You only wanted money. There's nothing unique about your story, Brooklyn. You're just like every other snake friend who ever walked the face of the earth. I thought we were better than this. I guess I was wrong."

"If I wanted you dead you wouldn't be here. It's important to know that. Yes, I fucked up. Yes, I moved foul, but I needed the cash."

I shook my head. He was totally arrogant, and it fucked me up. I would expect him to be more remorseful, but he wasn't. "You talk big shit. But it seems like you really don't know who I am."

166 BY MERCEDES BISHOP

"Miracle—."

"I can have you murdered, Brooklyn. And unlike me you'd never be found again."

He drank all of whatever was in his glass. Now I had him shook with visions of my father I'm sure. "I never got a chance to say I'm sorry."

"No, you didn't. And I'm waiting."

"I am." He shrugged. "We had bills and—."

"You're what?"

"Sorry."

I smiled. "Good. Because the first thing you gonna do is give me the money you got from my father."

His eyes widened and I could tell he took ownership of the funds as if he had the right. "But...but...I spent some of it already."

"What you got left?"

"Eighty grand."

I was angry but I'll take it. Besides, my father thinks the kidnappers dropped me off after the first one hundred thousand. I told him they had a change of heart. So, this money would be staying with me.

"Give me all of it and you'll owe me the rest."

He shook his head. "And what else?"

"Devon didn't come home last night. I think he's going to call off the wedding."

"He wouldn't do that. When you were gone, he was worried about you."

"I'm telling you that's exactly what he's going to do. But your job is to stop him. As a matter of fact, your sole responsibility is to convince him how stupid it would be to not go through with our ceremony."

"Devon is his own man. I can't make him do what he doesn't want to do. And I'm not even telling you that he doesn't want to marry you. To be honest he hasn't said anything to me about it."

"I know him. More than I know myself. I've been gone for a couple of days and what does he do? The moment I go see my father he uses the opportunity to leave the house. And you and I both know where he went."

"I don't know what you're talking about."

"So, you really want to play stupid? Nigga, I will ruin your fucking life!" When I slammed my fist on the bar a few people sitting around looked at us. "I'm tired of being nice to you. I want you to start respecting who I am and what I'm capable of."

He took a deep breath. "Okay, without saying I can do what you're asking, what happens if he does not want to be married? Have you given any real thought to that?"

"I will marry Devon. Even if I have to roll him down the aisle in a casket."

"Why is it so important?"

"You will help me; Brooklyn I promise you that!"

BROOKLYN

I was out all day thinking about Miracle. Prior to having her kidnapped, she was never really my favorite person. But now that she was forcing me to do something that I didn't want to, I can't lie, I started to despise her even more.

I was playing a video game at home when I got a call from an ex-girlfriend. She would've been my wife but after a year of dating she left me for another bitch. Her best friend. I spent four weeks letting this bitch lead me on and fuck with my mind. Telling me shit like, *I'm so confused. I think she's trying to turn me gay. But I want to be with you, Brooklyn.*

After a while her best friend met me at the bar and told me the truth. She let me know straight up that Karen had been with another girl for years. I'm not gonna lie, I don't hurt a lot in relationships, but that shit fucked me up.

After that point I stopped trusting women. Even if I was with them 24 hours a day in my mind they could still slide off and cheat if they wanted. I was smarter now about giving a female my whole heart.

Did I love Jamie? No, not really. But she was obedient and did what I asked when I asked. It got to a point where she was so dependent on my every word that for real, she started to be stupid.

"What's up with you?" Karen said in a seductive tone on the phone.

I sat back deeper in the sofa and put the game controller down. "Nothing much. What you been up to? Out there breaking other dude's hearts?" She was laughing but it wasn't a joke. I was dead serious. Pretty girls had a way of making a nigga lose reason and she was no different.

"Nope. I'm just being me. Been wondering what you've been up to? I mean, I used to see you at the bar, but you don't come around anymore."

"Why would I come around? That's your spot. Ain't that what you told me when we broke up?"

She laughed. "You know I didn't mean that shit."

"I never know what you mean. You don't express yourself."

"So, let me express myself now. I miss you. I'm sitting here drinking a little something and thinking about what we had in the past."

A set up was coming my way. "For real?"

"Yeah. How come it sounds like you don't believe me?"

"Maybe I don't."

"Brooklyn, if you don't wanna talk just say it and I'll let you go."

"Did I say all that?"

"Then why are you short with me?"

"Karen, I haven't heard from you in about two years. You hit me out of the blue. Don't a nigga got a right to ask a question?"

"You know what maybe I'll call you back when your attitude's better. Because — ."

"Don't hang up!" The second I said those words I hated myself for them. It wasn't until that moment that I really understood that she was the true love of my life. The one I let get away. The one I would do anything for. Even to this day.

"So, when can I see you?" She asked.

I moved a little in my seat. "I don't know. When you wanna see me?"

"What you doing later on tonight?"

"Nothing, I mean, I have a few errands to run. But beyond all that I'm good. What you wanna do?"

"You know what I wanna do. But you married and all."

My dick jumped. "Nah I don't know what you mean. You got to come out with it."

"Okay, well, I want to get a hotel room. Take a small radio with us. And listen to music as we make love. Do you remember how it used to be? Or am I the only one thinking about the past after all this time?"

She knew I remembered. That was how she got me hemmed up to begin with. We had a lot of problems in our relationship, but sex was not one of them. We would fight and break up. Have sex and get back together. I felt like a psycho and my addiction to this woman left me hating myself. Not because of how I felt. But because I couldn't let her go.

"Yeah, we can play that game. As long as it's worth my time."

"That sounds like a plan." She said. "Especially since I have some issues with my rent."

Damn! That's what this was all about? Her way of trying to get money out of my pockets? She had no cut cards. Gave no fucks about how it would make me feel. And just like it had always been in the past there was nothing I could do. I needed to see her. So, we exchanged details and I gave her a time of when we would meet.

A few minutes later Jamie came in the house. She was eating some candy and I looked at her for a moment. I hated her for gaining weight. I hated her for being weak. And I hated her for not having the strength enough to stand up to me. Don't get me wrong. I've always been a cheating type of nigga. But if she was just a little different, I don't think I would do it as much.

"You eating again?" I asked.

"It's just some M&M's."

"That's not what I asked you."

"I'm only eating them because you said you didn't want dinner. Said you weren't in the mood. So, I was going to go to—"

I stood up and within seconds was in her face. "Are you trying to get loud? And disrespect me? Are you jumping bad like I won't fuck you up in here?"

Her eyes widened. "Brooklyn, I don't wanna fight. I was only saying that I was eating candy because—."

"I heard what you said! And you still not getting it! Are you breaking bad with me or not?"

Before she answered I punched her in the stomach. Pieces of candy and whatever else she ate came flying out of her mouth. I don't know how long it was, but I beat her until I felt relief. At some point I no longer saw her face. I saw my mother's. I saw the girl who disrespected me at the food depot when we were purchasing products for the truck. But most of all I saw Karen.

When I was done, I said, "I'm sorry. But you left me no choice."

CHAPTER, MARRIED TO THE DRAMA

12

DEVON

I was sitting in my house trying to figure out what I wanted to do with my life. Miracle was in the other room and I know she wanted to talk about one thing. Her kidnapping. In her mind I didn't care enough. But how does she know what I'm thinking? She always jumps to conclusions. Which was super annoying.

When she walked out of the room she was fully dressed. Which I was happy about because it meant she was leaving the house. Evident by the LV purse she was carrying.

"You going out?" I asked even though I didn't care.

"Yeah. Later. But are we going to talk about what I went through?"

"I thought you didn't wanna talk about it. I thought you said it was still fresh. The last thing I wanna do is make things worse for you."

"The last thing you wanna do? Are you serious?"

"What that supposed to mean?" I crossed my arms over my chest.

"I would think the last thing you wanna do is see me get killed. I went through a lot this week, Devon! Don't you understand that? Or are you that selfish where you don't care?"

"I know what you're doing." I pointed at her. "And I'm not gonna let you take me there."

"What am I doing?" She continued throwing her hands up. "The only thing I want is a connection with my fiancé. Is that too much to ask?"

What was she still doing here? I thought she was bouncing. "Miracle, when you come back, we'll talk."

She shook her head and walked out the door. I was so glad she was gone. I was about to roll up some weed when someone knocked at the door about fifteen minutes later. It was Brooklyn.

I opened the door to let him inside, shaking his hand weakly. "I thought you were sick?"

"What you talking about?"

I knew the nigga was lying. "You said you couldn't show up at the food truck because you were sick. So, what you doing here?"

He coughed once. "Oh, I feel better now. Was just stopping by to see what you were up to with Miracle."

"She blowing me, man! I was concerned when she first was gone but now, I'm realizing it was probably the best thing that could've happen to me. Because I was finally able to get some fucking rest."

"Did she say what happened?"

"Nah...just some niggas got her. Fuck that bitch."

"Come on, man. You have to be a little more sensitive than that. The girl was kidnapped."

"What that got to do with me?"

He frowned. "What it got to do with you? She needs you now. You don't go through what she's going through without scars. Maybe you should be a little more sensitive."

This nigga sounded stupid. I didn't owe her anything, especially not sympathy. I wasn't the one who took her. I was the one her father tried to kill, just 'cause I knew the bitch. "Riddle me this, why are you so concerned?"

"Not concerned." He shrugged.

"You sure though?"

"Listen, I saw how fucked up you were when you came to my house with your —."

"You wanna know something, when I stopped by, I thought you were involved with all this shit."

He glared. "Me? Why?"

"For starters I saw some weird ass nigga yelling at you. Seemed off."

"So, because some nigga who was on drugs stopped by my crib, I was involved? I thought you knew me better than that."

I folded my arms. "At this point I don't know who to trust."

"It's simple." He moved closer. "If I was involved, she would have told you. So, do you trust me or not?"

I was silent. Not trying to be rude, but I wasn't really sure. "Yeah. Maybe."

I wasn't sure but for some reason he exhaled loudly. Like he was holding his breath. Which to me was kind of weird. "Okay, if you trust me then here this, that woman needs you right now."

I laughed.

"What's funny?" He continued.

"You beat your wife and you giving me advice?"

He squared up and I did too. If we were gonna bust down, he wasn't gonna catch me slipping.

"I don't beat her. I put her in her place, there's a difference." He relaxed his stance.

"I fuck with you like a brother. But you can't tell me about a woman with your record. We can talk about food. Bitches and hos. But anything pertaining to a relationship, and how to treat a woman is out of your league."

"Say what you want."

"I will. Because I don't know who you are right now, but you definitely giving me the wrong vibes."

"You know what, do whatever you want! I'm out of here."

JAMIE

I don't know how it was possible, but I made it out of my apartment and down the steps. Every time I inhaled and exhaled, I felt severe pain in my rib area. I knew something was wrong, but I didn't know what.

After walking down the steps, which felt like forever, I approached my car. It was at that time that I realized I didn't have my car keys. After he beat me, Brooklyn wasn't anywhere to be found but I was sure he was coming home soon. Probably with some food and roses. Something he always did after he'd gone too far.

For me, this time felt different.

I was no longer interested in being used and abused. I was no longer interested in being his punching bag. I hate that it took me this long to come to an understanding with myself. And more than anything I hope I'm being for real this time. I know my friends and family get frustrated with me. Sometimes I say I'll leave, but I never really do. But how do you break up with someone who's been your entire life?

Everyone has an opinion on what I should be doing. And some of the advice is good. But I need help. Help in getting out of my relationship. But more than anything help in getting out of my relationships safely. And alive. Which was two different things all together. And most of the time all people had were reasons and not enough plans.

When I turned around and looked at my door, I realized going inside to get my keys would be next to impossible. There was no way I could crawl all the way up the steps again. Not without severe pain. Because even as I leaned against the car door it was like someone was driving several hot fire sticks into my body. Out of all of the times he beat me this was the worst.

And I was really sure, it would be the last.

At least I hoped.

TAMMY

I was sitting in my car outside of Carson's house trying to convince myself to go inside. No scratch that, trying to convince myself to knock on the door. Because there were no guarantees that he would let me in. And why should he?

Everything my mother said was correct. How I favored madness. Because sitting in my home or sitting in my car by myself would force me to listen to my own thoughts. And there is nothing or no one harder on me than myself.

After deciding to go home I ducked down when I saw Carson pulling up in a new luxury truck. I guess he bought it to make the move to Georgia. The thing was I also saw someone moving in the passenger seat although I couldn't see the person's face. When Carson parked in his spot at that time, I got a better view. It was a woman. How could he move on that quickly? It hadn't even been a whole week. Was I that replaceable?

When they were leaving the truck I quickly got out of my car. The moment he saw me he threw her the keys and said, "Wait inside for me."

I moved closer. "Who is that?"

"What you doing here?"

"We weren't together long but this is how you do me? You shack up with another bitch not even a week after we break up?"

"I told you I was done." He shrugged.

"But I'm not done with us."

"That doesn't have anything to do with me."

"Why, Carson?" As if I didn't know all the reasons he should cut me off.

"For starters I don't trust you. And the way you been acting, I don't even like you. So why should I keep you on my arm?"

Suddenly my stomach hurt. I don't know what I expected when I got here but it definitely wasn't to see him with another girl. Not only did he have a lackadaisical attitude, but he didn't seem to care.

Why didn't he care?

"You should have me on your arm because I love you. You should have me on your arm because we are perfect together. Don't you see that? Or are you that blind that everything misses you?"

"I want you off my property. I won't say it again."

I could tell he was serious. He was actually done with me. And it wore me out more than I realized. It's one thing to take a person for advantage. It's a whole different matter when they leave you and you realize you are really alone.

"I'm not giving you your money back."

He chuckled once. "Did I ask for it back?"

"I'm just letting you know, Carson! Now I realize you were trying to control me with your money! I wish I never accepted it! I wish I never allowed myself to be used by you. To think that this was actually a real relationship. You never had any intentions on doing right by me. It was all a game. Tell the truth!"

He looked at me one final time and said the words I never wanted to hear. "The best thing I could have ever done was drop you. Goodbye, bitch. It's over." He walked away.

TAMMY

I was devastated after leaving Carson's place. I felt so stupid because it was mainly my fault. He left me because I couldn't decide what I wanted. I couldn't decide if my friends were more important than my relationship. It doesn't matter now because he made the decision for me.

I needed to move on.

I needed Devon.

I parked my car when I saw Devon about to get into his truck. I beeped a few times and he saw me before walking my way. He pulled my car door open and slid into the passenger seat. "You almost missed me. I was just about to roll out."

"I can come by a different time if you want me to."

"No! I mean, you don't have to go."

He looked down and I felt like he wanted to say something else. Devon always had deep moments, but this felt different. It was like he was searching inside of himself for something else. What that thing was I didn't know.

"I got to tell you something." He said. "And I don't want you to be scared because that's the last thing I need when you look at me."

"But you're scaring me now." I admitted.

"Don't be afraid. That's not what I wanna do here. I just, kinda wanna be real with you. Realer than I ever been before. It's just that if you not feeling what I'm about to say I don't want you to run either."

"Ok." My stomach jumped a little. "I'm listening."

"Ever since I've known you, I always felt like our relationship was deeper than we let on. That so much more was happening between us and that we were afraid to go with the flow. And I know I sound crazy but almost losing Miracle made things clearer to me." He laughed. "To be honest things are clearer than they've ever been."

"I mean is she ok? You guys are good right?"

"Yeah, but this ain't about that. This is about—."

Suddenly my phone rang, and I was irritated. I knew off the break that he wanted to say something at that moment and the call may have ruined it all. Still, I answered it for whatever reason.

It was Jamie.

"What up with you? I'm kind of busy right—."

"I'm at the hospital. I need you to come. And please don't put me off. You're the only friend I got."

CHAPTER, ENEMIES
BECOME FRIENDS
13
JAMIE

The nurse just came in to check my vitals and I suddenly started crying. She was so attentive and delicate with me that it became obvious that I had never *really* been touched by my husband. There was nothing sexual about her affection. I'm sure it was all business. But that didn't stop it from feeling genuine and making me feel better.

"Do you need anything else? Are you in any pain?" She asked as she looked down at me with a smile on her face.

I shook my head no although I desperately desired her to stay longer. And yes, I'm fully aware that asking her to do so would've seemed creepy. Would have seen weirder. I'm sure a lot of people come in here damaged and needing attention. And if I was wild enough to ask her to stay, I'm sure she would have smiled.

"I'm fine. Thank you."

She nodded and walked away.

BY MERCEDES BISHOP

I was just about to get some rest when Tammy came through the door. The moment she saw my face she covered her mouth with both hands. I already knew it was bad. But her expression told me it was worse than I thought. I'm sure by now the blue hues under my brown skin had begun to show.

There was no doubt in my mind although I tried to knock it for many years that I was a bad wife. The one who ran away when anybody assumed that my husband was beating me.

She walked deeper into the room and the first thing she did was hold my hand. She didn't ask me what happened. She didn't need the details. It was as if she had learned in the brief time, we separated how to be a true friend. Or maybe she always knew, and I couldn't see it.

After 15 minutes it was I who broke the silence. "I'm going to leave him this time, Tammy."

She squeezed my hand. And smiled. "That's good."

"I'm serious. I'm tired of getting hurt like this. Although I must admit this was the worst he'd ever beaten me."

"Okay, so do you have a plan?"

"I don't right now. But I know I can't move back in the house. I don't think I can face him again even if it was for me to pack my clothes. And at the same time, I don't have enough money to run away from it all." I sniffled. "And even if I did where would I go? I'm not the kind of girl who is strong by herself." I wiped a few tears away that were streaming down my face. "I need a man."

"What if I told you I have a plan?" She said. "I mean it's dumb, but I think if we put our minds together it might work."

"What is it, Tammy?" I could feel my heart pumping.

"Before I tell you, I want you to be sure. Are you sure?"

I put my hand over my heart. "I've never been surer."

She took a deep breath. "I don't want to hear a few days down the line that you miss Brooklyn and you have to see him again."

"You're making me nervous. Just tell me what the idea is."

"I want to get away too. I want to leave everything behind and go someplace different. Someplace where people don't know me. I kind of want to start all over. And maybe we can do that together."

"I'm confused. Because your plan doesn't sound like it involves me. It actually doesn't sound like a plan at all."

"Let's get an apartment together. Out of state. Someplace like Atlanta." She shrugged. "To be honest I don't care where we go. As long as we leave."

It was like a dream come true. "I'm ready when you are."

JAMIE

Well…we didn't make it to Georgia.

We moved to Virginia because we realized going too far may be a little too scary for both of us. But I was having so much fun with her. It felt good to get up and go about my day without having to worry if I said or did the wrong thing to Brooklyn.

We settled on a cute little two-bedroom apartment. That was designed in a roommate fashion. She had her own space and her own bathroom. And I had my own space and my own bathroom. But for some reason we enjoyed each other's company, so we slept in the same room.

We ate breakfast for dinner. And dinner for breakfast. We watched movies back to back as if we were two high school girls sleeping over each other's houses. We laughed and told each other secrets. I told her how I met Brooklyn and how I cared about him before I knew how to care about myself. And she told me about Carson and how much she missed and loved him. Although she was sure it was mostly because he didn't want her anymore.

There was no end to what we wouldn't tell one another. It was like we were always good friends who didn't know until we decided to be bold and jump full fledge into life. And when I was scared about being alone for the first time in a long time, she cried with me and made me feel like everything would be ok. And I was ok. I was rebuilding my strength.

And then he called and ruined everything.

And I was alone in our apartment.

"Jamie! Look, I know you're on the other line and I know you don't want to speak to me." Brooklyn said. "So, you don't have to. Just hear me out. Just listen to what I'm about to say. And if you don't want to hear from me anymore, I'll never call you again."

I remained quiet too afraid to say something that would put me back in connection with him. So, I sat on the sofa trembling as if he could see me. Trembling as if he could beat me again.

"I'm a man. But I'm also a stupid man. I took you for granted in the worst way. You trusted me and I rewarded you by beating you every chance I got. But it wasn't your fault. It was mine. I'm weak and because I never knew how to love I could never love you right. But please give me another chance. Please let me show you I can be the husband you need. That I can be the husband you deserve. That's all I'm asking for. And I'll never bother you again."

When he was done, I wiped the tears from my eyes and took a deep breath. This moment would change everything. And I knew it. So, I had to be careful and I had to be sure.

"Baby, please come home! I'm nothing without you. I haven't even left the house since you been gone. Devon keeps asking me if I'm going to work the truck but how can I when all I can think about is my wife?"

"Brooklyn..."

"Come home and talk to me!"

"Never call me again!" I hung up.

TAMMY

I felt bad about this but technically I wasn't breaking any promise to Jamie. Still, we told each other we would stay away from everybody in Maryland until it was the right time. Not just the right time for us physically but the right time for us mentally.

And still here I was sitting in Devon's apartment in Maryland, trying to get him to finish saying what was on his mind. To finish saying whatever he was going to tell me before Jamie called and let me know she was in the hospital.

"I'm glad you came by." He said running his hands down the gray sweats he wore. He smelled as if he just stepped out of the shower. "You want anything to drink?"

"You have soda? Anything sweet really."

He walked toward the kitchen and suddenly he stopped. His back was faced me so I didn't know what he was about to say. Or what he was thinking. Slowly he turned around and looked at me.

"I don't understand why you would leave like that."
He remained where he was standing.

"I had to get away." I shrugged.

"But you didn't stop to think how that would make me feel? After everything that happened with Miracle. You were wrong, Tammy! I thought someone hurt you! And then you not answering your phone. What kind of shit is that?"

"It wasn't about you, Devon. It was about me needing to do something for myself!" I placed my hand over my heart. "Don't you get that?"

"Nah, I don't. I was fucked up when nobody heard from you. Went over that nigga Carson's house and everything."

When he said he went to Carson's, I moved uneasily in my seat. "You went by Carson's house?"

"That's what I just said."

"What did he say?"

"Are you serious?"

"I'm just asking."

"And I didn't invite you here for all that."

I sighed for what seemed like forever. "Devon, tell me what's on your mind because I'm confused."

He took a deep breath and sat next to me. "I'm in love with you. I've always been in love with you. And I know that's hard for you to understand. You might not even care. But I have to be real with how I feel."

My heartbeat so loudly I could feel it pulsating in my ear. "How long have you felt like this? I mean, you never said anything to me before. You, you, you, never, never..."

He walked over to me and placed his hand on my thigh. "You don't have to be scared."

I got up and walked to the other side of the living room. I don't know if I expected this. Maybe a part of me knew this would come up. And at the same time, it messed me up so much that I couldn't think straight.

"Tammy, you have to tell me something."

"I'm..." Nothing would come out.

"I just told you I love you and all you can do is stand over there and look crazy?"

"Well what do you want me to say?"

"It's simple. Either you love me, or you don't. So, do you?"

I thought long and hard. I thought about our history. I didn't want things to change just because we decided to *be together*. And at the same time, I would be lying to myself if I didn't admit that Carson was always a substitute. He was always something to do when I couldn't be with Devon. But we spent all of our lives

194   BY MERCEDES BISHOP

never crossing boundaries. What would that mean if things changed now?

I walked over and sat next to him. Taking a deep breath, I said, "I do love you. And, and, I think I always knew. But was afraid that things would change between us if I admitted my feelings. I thought it would come up when we spent the time together in the hotel room...but we just fell back into being safe. But now I'm realizing if we are going to do this then things have to change."

He reached over and kissed me. And I can't lie, it was like he had the key to my heart. My body warmed up. My hands trembled. I felt dizzy and unsure. And despite it all it felt right.

When our lips separated for a moment, before he kissed me lightly again, I asked, "So, what now?"

"I want us to move in together. I want us to have the life that we deserve. I have some things in the working too."

"What does that mean?"

"I'm going to sell my truck. That should give us enough money to —."

I leaned my head back. "Sell your truck? You can't do that!"

"That truck doesn't mean anything to me."

"You're lying. I remember before you started the business. You loved to cook for fun."

"That was then."

"But a dream is still a dream, Devon. What's really going on?"

He looked down. "You're right. I do love the truck. But I can't afford to take care of it anymore. It's time for me to put the dream aside and get a job. Because I want to walk into our life together without worrying about bills or problems. I want to take care of you."

"But you built that business from the ground up, Devon. You don't walk away as if it doesn't matter."

"You and me, that's all I care about right now."

"Right now?"

"Forever."

I smiled. Because I can tell in his eyes that he was being honest. At the same time what start would we have if every time he gets upset, he can walk away. "Okay, maybe we should—."

KNOCK. KNOCK. KNOCK

We both jumped as if we were doing something wrong. Maybe we were. "Who's that?"

He walked over to the door and looked out the peephole. Slowly his head turned toward mine. "It's Penny." He whispered.

"You have to open the door. Your truck is out front."

Slowly he did and Penny walked inside. He looked at me and smiled. I think he liked me despite how Miracle felt but I couldn't be sure. Still, he gave everybody else a hard time but for some reason I was on his good side.

"Hi, Mr. Penny." I said.

He winked and focused his attention on Devon. "Listen, I want to talk to you about the situation with Miracle."

I moved toward the door, preparing to leave.

"You don't have to go anywhere." Penny said. "This will be quick."

I sat back down.

"I never got to thank you for doing everything you could for my daughter. I know things were rough and I should have looked into the matter deeply, instead of giving you such a hard time. And even though you lost 100 grand, Miracle made it clear that you deserve my respect for at least trying to get her back."

"I, I don't know what to say."

"Don't say anything. Just listen. I'm gonna give you the money you need to expand your truck business. It'll be in the joint account you share with Miracle. And with that money I want you to marry my daughter and to be the husband I know you can be."

"So, like a, I mean, bribe?"

He stepped closer. "Don't bite the hand that gives. You will marry her."

I looked down and I felt my stomach swirling. And Devon looked at me.

"Ok, ok, sir."

No longer able to sit by and have my feelings hurt I got up and walked out the door. They both called my name, but I was already gone.

Taking the long trip back to Virginia, tears welled up in my eyes. I hate that I allowed myself to feel something. I knew I would be in a bad mood all day. But when I got back home Jamie was so happy to see me. She had made lasagna, all vegetables with a great sauce and cheese mix.

Just being around her and this newfound happy mood she possessed allowed me to momentarily forget about everything. I didn't tell her about seeing Devon. I didn't want to ruin the vibe. Besides, I'm not the girl who gets happy endings. I'm the one who sits by and watches everyone thrive.

I'm the one who loves Madness.

CHAPTER, NOT FAR ENOUGH

14

TAMMY

NEXT DAY

I decided many things. The main thing I decided was that I didn't move far enough away. I know some people say you can't run from your troubles, but I don't believe them. You can't tell me that someone born in poverty won't have a better chance if they move to the suburbs. You can't tell me that someone living around pollution won't breathe better where the air is cleaner.

I needed to move further.

When I made it to our apartment in preparation to leave Virginia, I was surprised that Jamie was there. She told me earlier that she wanted to get her hair and nails done. Something she hadn't done in a while for fear that Brooklyn would be mad. So why was she at home now?

"I didn't think you would be here." I put my purse on the table. "You didn't make your nail appointment?"

"I wasn't much in the mood. I mean, I got a call the other day and I think it's still bothering me a little. And I know it's fucked up, but I got to be real."

"It was Brooklyn?"

She nodded yes. "Don't get me wrong I know we don't need to be together. But it doesn't stop how I feel."

"I'm not judging you. Even if I want to, I have no room."

"So, what's up with you?" She patted the bed once. I sat next to her. "You look kind of sad."

"I want to move further away, Jamie. I want to go further out of town mainly because I don't trust myself."

"Okay so where are we going to go?"

"Let's move to Atlanta. We talked about doing it before, but we got scared. I'm not scared anymore."

She said yes.

I was surprised it was that simple. I guess talking to Brooklyn made her uneasy. It's always easier giving in when the person is close. But when you have to drive and put in more effort things become harder.

So, we ran. Away from Brooklyn. Away from Carson. And away from Devon.

We already broke the lease at one apartment and had no intentions on doing the same here in Atlanta. So, we got a hotel room to chill a little while until we found one we really liked. We were throwing money away, by we, I mean me. But I felt it was worth it in the long run.

We were sitting on the bed eating pizza when I looked over at her. Wiping my mouth with the back of my hand I asked, "How did he start?"

"Brooklyn?"

I nodded.

"I can't remember the exact day he first hit me. Because there were so many little things leading up to that point. He would make a comment and I would speak out on it. And if he didn't agree with me, he would yell or scream. It's so funny to look at it now because just hearing his voice raised used to be enough to make me cry. But I got tough, I guess. And so, his rants didn't bother me anymore. So, he kicked it up a notch."

"You don't have to talk about it if you don't want, Jamie. Like for real. I know this is hard. It's just that, I kinda always wanted to know why you stayed."

"I don't mind talking about it." She looked down at the pizza in her hand and put it on the bed. "If I think harder, I believe the first time I can remember that he hit me it was on my birthday. Back when I had more friends outside of just our group."

"I had gotten so many gifts that it was tough to see the floor where they sat. And I remember looking at his face and seeing what I thought was jealousy. Jealousy that I was shining. Jealousy that I was happy. And jealousy probably because for the moment he couldn't make me sad without looking like the villain."

She looked as if she wanted to cry and suddenly, I felt stupid for bringing it up. "I'm so sorry."

"So, he took me in the back." She continued. "Told me he wanted to give me his gift. I was so excited about everything that I couldn't see his eyes. It's only now that I play the tapes back, but I can remember it. But I couldn't see his eyes or the hate he had for me in that moment. Anyway, he closed the door and punched me in my stomach. He learned that bruises couldn't be shown below the neck. So, he was careful. When he was done, I remember thinking oh my God I married a monster."

"So, what did you do?"

"I sat there for five minutes. He wouldn't let me leave even if I wanted to go back out with my friends. He told me not to go back out without a smile on my face. I think that was the first time I became a partner in his crimes toward me. And I believe that's also a reason why I don't want to be with him now."

"Why you say that?"

"Because I believe he tried to kill me recently. Like he wanted me dead. And if I stay this time, I'll be a partner with him in my death."

It was so crazy. I was learning more about her. And without Brooklyn around or Carson, or Devon, I was able to stop being so judgmental. And to understand how difficult it was for her to let anyone know about the abuse.

"Now, you tell me, why are you and Devon not together?"

The pizza almost went flying out of my mouth. How was she able to know what I was feeling when I didn't? "What are you talking about?"

"Don't play games. I know you're in love with him."

"I don't know what you think is going on between me and Devon, but we've never been anything more than friends. I don't even look at him like that."

"I don't believe either of you knew how you felt. But it doesn't mean you aren't in love. So, tell me...do you know now?"

I thought about being honest with her. But even though Devon and I discussed the possibility of being together, we didn't go there.

"Devon and I have only ever been friends. Don't get me wrong, we're close and it's usually hard for people to understand how a man and a woman can be friends. But that's their hang-up not ours. He is a friend now and he'll be a friend to me always."

She shrugged. "If you say so." She grabbed her pizza and began to eat.

Ten minutes later my phone was ringing again. Devon had been calling nonstop, but I wasn't interested in speaking to him. He and I both knew what receiving the money from Penny meant for our relationship. It meant that he would have to go through with the marriage to Miracle. It meant he would have to build a future with her and for her. A future that would not concern me.

I was finally understanding that a married man could not be my best friend. And the thought of this, just trying to understand it all, ripped me apart. In ways I wouldn't allow myself to express.

At least for now.

DEVON

I was not feeling this tuxedo. It wasn't enough for me to make a commitment, Miracle had to control every aspect of how I looked at this wedding. Everything had to be crisp. Everything had to be neat. And there was no room for not even a hair out of place.

After making sure my Tuxedo fit, I waited for my friends. I didn't bother hitting up Brooklyn. He made it clear that he didn't want to fuck with me so why should I fuck with him? So, it tripped me out when he was the first person who walked through the door.

"Why you looking all crazy?" Brooklyn asked.

"Because I didn't think you would come."

"Why wouldn't I?" He shrugged. "I mean I'm still your best man, right?"

I shook my head. "So, we gonna pretend we didn't have a—."

"What are we, girls?"

"What, nigga?"

"So, you ain't like something I said." He shrugged. "So, you wasn't feeling what I was feeling. So now we beefing?"

I started to say yes. But I thought about it longer. I've been knowing this dude for a minute. And it was stupid to beef with him. So, I shook his hand instead.

"How are you feeling?" He walked over to the suits. "About everything now?"

"You really wanna know?"

"I'm your friend before I'm hers."

"Well I'm still not feeling the wedding. But after Penny gave me that paper, I ain't got no choice."

"Penny gave you cash?"

"Yep. Well, in our joint account. I was gonna close the truck business, but he came through.

"You asked him?"

"Nah, he just brought the paper out of the blue."

"You one lucky as nigga."

"That's one way to look at it."

"However you look at it I'm just glad he gave you the money. Between me and you I was looking forward to the chain thing you were talking about. I figured we can have a truck in DC, New York, Atlanta, so to me ain't no reason to shut it down now."

He was talking but for real I wasn't listening. The wedding was Saturday and I already felt like it was too soon. But he was right about some things, there was really no way out. Not without dying.

DEVON

Making love to her felt like I was having sex with a plastic doll. She didn't move, she didn't moan, she barely said anything. She would complain in the past about our sexual relationship, but she applied no effort. Normally I would be picking up her slack. Kissing her. Telling her I loved her. Anything I could do to get us both there so I could go to sleep. But tonight, was different. I didn't feel like helping out. I didn't feel like doing anything.

So, I fucked her lightly. And then when she tapped my shoulder, letting me know she came, I got up and laid on my side. With my back in her direction.

"Wow…what's wrong with you?" She asked adjusting the sheets.

"Nothing. Just tired." I yawned long and hard.

"You don't act like you're tired. You act like you have an attitude."

I shook my head.

"Devon, it seems like since I've been gone you've been more distant. When are you going to come back to me mentally? When are you going to act like a fiancé and not a prostitute?"

"I'm sorry…are we talking about having sex or are we talking about our future marriage?"

"Let me put it like this I know you're in love with your best friend."

My eyes widened and I turned around to face her. "I'm not in love with Tammy. We just cool. You know that."

"I know you're treating me worse than a dog. I know you don't want to be here. And I know my father gave you a lot of money. So technically, if I were you, I'd treat me a little nicer."

"Hold up, you're threatening me?"

"I don't have time to threaten you. You've been paid to make a life with me and that's what I expect you to do. Oh, and don't forget to put the truck business in my name too. Like my daddy says, now we're partners."

CHAPTER, BROKEN STRINGS

15

· TAMMY

After staying in our hotel room for days we decided it was best to go out and have a good time. It was my idea actually and the moment I had to get dressed I realized I didn't feel like going out. Luckily for me Jamie wouldn't hear of it.

She planned everything out. What she was going to wear. What I was going to wear. And where we were going to go. Literally all I had to do was get up and take a shower and throw on my clothes. Oh, I also had to give her my credit card which at this point was down $4000 of the money that Carson gave me.

At first, I was kind of bummed. Like I said, I didn't feel like going. But the moment I saw the club I grew excited. It's amazing how when you live in a bubble you think only in terms of what you can see. But when you go out and experience the world, your eyes widen.

After posting up against the wall for about an hour and bopping our heads to the music we finally happened upon a table for two. There were drink glasses and balled up napkins all over the place, but it didn't bother us. We just put the things on the floor and continued to dance in place.

"I can't believe how nice this club is!" She yelled to be heard over the music. "I think we should've come along time ago!"

I heard her but I was too busy looking at the two guys who were staring in our direction. One of them was tall and butter colored like Carson. And the other had the complexion of milk chocolate. They both looked edible and either one would have been fine with me.

"What you looking at?"

"Don't turn your head too quickly but there are two guys who have been staring at us since we got in here. I think they about to come over. Although I wish it would be sooner than later."

Instead of doing what I asked, she looked directly at them and smiled so widely she resembled The Joker. Both of them grinned and nodded back before walking toward us.

"Why you do that?" I asked. "Now you got us looking like whores!"

"Listen, we in town without a permanent date. And I've been without my husband for weeks. I also have been without another man but him forever. If I had Carson's fine ass, I may be fine with playing hard to get. But I don't and I want to finally have some fun. I hate when bitches put on airs instead of having a good time!"

And have a good time is what she did. From the moment the guys walked over to us, their names being Josh and Oakland, she went on and on without giving them a chance to speak. I was starting to believe they enjoyed her conversation.

I also got a chance to see her personality at play. Men gravitated toward her. They seemed enamored with her, which caused me extreme confusion. You have to understand Jamie isn't the kind of person in our circle to get a lot of attention. So, what was it about her now?

"What about you?" Josh asked me. He had the butter complexion. "You seem really quiet over there." He smiled and his teeth were shiny white. This was a man who took care of himself.

I sipped on an empty straw. "Ain't nothing up. Just listening to you two."

"So, you antisocial?"

"I wouldn't say all that. I'm just not the kind of person who talks more than I listen that's all."

"I get it now." He nodded. "You're trying to feel me out. To make sure I'm not crazy." He pointed a manicured nail at me. "I like females like you. Chicks these days go on and on about how this girl or that girl is jealous of them. But that doesn't seem like your style. I know you gotta have a man."

I thought about my situation. Not only did I not have a man I didn't have anyone who was sincerely interested in me. Not that I should throw a pity party. It's definitely of my own doing. But that doesn't make me less lonely.

"Nah, I'm single."

"I plan on changing that if you let me." He grabbed himself and I thought it was strange. Was he just readjusting or being nasty?

I mean how does he intend on changing that? By fucking me? This is why I can't with some guys. They always think in terms of what they want physically. And never in terms of what females need.

When he first started talking to me, I had hopes he could help pass the time. But now I'm not so sure.

But when I looked over at Jamie, she seemed to be having the time of her life. She was laughing at him hard and heavy and I could tell in her eyes that thoughts of Brooklyn were long gone. I wish I could be like that.

Three hours later we were in a hotel room not too far from ours. She continued to talk and continued to laugh at weak jokes. At this point she flirted with both of them. While I was sitting on a chair by the desk watching. Josh no longer made any attempts to include me in on the conversation. He didn't make any attempt to even look my way. I was, for the first time in my life, really invisible.

And then the strangest thing happened. Jamie walked over to me and grabbed me by my hand, taking me into the bathroom. When the door was closed, she said, "I can see you're not feeling Josh are you?"

"I mean, should I?" I leaned against the sink.

"I think you should." She shrugged. "He's making all efforts to get to know you. I thought we were both going to loosen up tonight?"

"Jamie, what is this about?"

"You mind if I fuck both of them?"

I heard her but I thought I was having an out of body experience. You have to understand, this is not the Jamie I knew. She was mostly always with Brooklyn. They were friends first. We all were. But then their friendship went to marriage and I didn't know her to have anyone else.

"I think I'm tripping." I stood up straight. "Did you just say you wanted to fuck both of them? Because I know I didn't hear what I thought I heard."

"I hate when you act all judgmental."

"How is that being judgmental? You don't even know these niggas. And now you're saying you want to fuck both of them?"

She had no time for my questions. She asked me again if I wanted to be with Josh and I said no. After that, she exited the bathroom and left me inside. And there I stayed, like a child for fifteen minutes until I heard moaning.

When I opened the door, I saw her in the middle of two men. Two strangers. She was sucking one of their dicks while the other fucked her from behind.

The thing that fucked me up the most was that she seemed comfortable. Like she done this many times before. I knew then that I had to get rid of her. I just didn't know how.

DEVON

It was supposed to be my bachelor party, but I was annoyed. Who came up with this stupid shit anyway? I wasn't interested in celebrating a marriage to a woman

BY MERCEDES BISHOP

I couldn't stand. But nobody seemed interested in how I felt. And no one seemed to care.

I was just another reason for people to have a party. For people to move around me like I wasn't there.

Damn, I missed Tammy.

I miss her more than I was willing to let on. But what could I say?

"You good, nigga?" Brooklyn asked walking up to me with a glass of something dark in his hand.

I nodded.

"The strippers gonna be here in a minute." He took a deep sip.

I frowned. "Okay, so where they at?"

"I said they coming now. Stop rushing." He looked at me harder. "You sure you good?"

"I keep telling you I'm fine." He was getting on my nerves but at this point I was used to it. I don't understand how he was supposed to be my friend but doesn't get me. Everything in me said I didn't want to marry this bitch. Even she knew it.

Fifteen minutes later the women had arrived and to be honest I was pleasantly surprised. One of them was really cute. The kind a girl I could be into. The other one not so much but her body was on point. To be honest I don't care what they look like at this point. Their bodies were a welcomed distraction. I didn't want to be thinking about getting married. I wanted to be thinking about my life in a way that was different from what it is now.

I wanted to be thinking about Tammy.

When the strippers finished doing their sets, the one with the pretty face and good enough body walked over to me. She whispered exactly what I wanted to hear in my ear.

A minute later I was following her to a room off the side of the club. I knew about the spot. It's the place where you went if you wanted a little extra fun. And I wanted a little extra. I wanted a lot. So, I sat in a chair in the middle of the floor. And she walked up to me. Looking and smelling good.

"Any requests?" She asked.

I fell back in the chair. "Nah, mami. I'm gonna let you do your thing."

The first thing she did was grab a pillow that sat in the corner of the room. I hadn't noticed it before. I guess I didn't care. Placing the pillow before me she dropped to her knees. When I looked down at the purple pillow, I could tell there was a spot where the material had worn off. She'd done this many times using the same pillow. And again, I didn't care.

Within one minute my dick was in her mouth. Her tongue was warm and wet. How did she do that? Out of all the blowjobs I received I never experienced a sensation like this in my life. It ran through me. Caused me to feel things I didn't know existed. I knew then that if I wasn't careful, I would be seeing her again.

Hold up. What was her name?

It didn't matter. Our situation was born out of necessity. I needed the sensation and she needed the money. Together we were a match made in lust.

She clearly wasn't done with me. She did this thing I loved where with my dick in her mouth, she looked up at me. Begging me with her eyes for more, as if my dick held nectar that would make her younger, sexier, and finer. This woman knew how to seduce, and I loved her for it. Not in a creepy way. But in a way I liked.

She went on and on for five minutes. And let's be clear, I came twice. I don't know what made her so interested in me. I'm pretty sure Brooklyn or one of my other groomsmen paid her off.

But this was good. This was great. Finally, a gift I wanted. Finally, a gift I could use. After this night I would reconsider everything. And that included marrying Miracle.

There would be no more allowing her to lay in bed like a corpse. No more allowing her to make me do all the work. If I was forced to marry her, she would fuck me like I wanted. Fuck me like I needed. Or I would be the worst husband she ever had. I'm talking about the ultimate disrespectful type nigga. The kind that consistently worked to make her cry.

After we did our thing in the smaller room, I walked back out into the party area. Brooklyn and the rest of my men were smiling. I knew what they were thinking. My total expression had changed. I was no longer uptight. I decided that if this was my bachelor party, if this was the end of life as I knew it, I might as well have fun.

So, I drank, smoked and danced. And when I was horny again, I grabbed the girl, the unnamed one, and took her into the room. She never refused. Again, she gave me those eyes.

This was life.

So why was I still thinking about Tammy?

MIRACLE

I was talking to Brooklyn on the phone trying to get the details of Devon's party. After all, I was paying for everything. I know some people thought it was dumb that I did so much in our relationship. But I have my reasons for sticking around so long.

For starters there was no way in the world that I would allow him to be with who I think he wants to be with. Tammy and Devon could fake all day like they didn't fuck. But I know that's why they spent so much time together. And you don't get to walk into my life and use me. Nah, he was going to marry me.

"I don't care if he's having a good time now, Brooklyn. Did he like the girl I paid for or not?" I asked as I stood outside of my bachelorette party in a restaurant in Washington D.C.

"I can tell you this, he had a smile on his face after he went into the room the first time and came out the fourth."

I don't know but for some reason I was annoyed. Yeah this was kind of like a set up. Yes, I made sure the girl found and took pictures of everything he did to violate our upcoming vows. Still, it hurts my heart that he didn't even consider not being with her. That he didn't even consider cheating on me. I bet you that had I been Tammy it would've been a whole different story.

"Keep an eye on him, Brooklyn! Don't forget you owe me!"

"I wish I could forget it. Because to be honest, I'm tired of you throwing it up in my face every five minutes."

"If I were you, I'd be a little more grateful. Because if I tell my father what you did you wouldn't have a face at all."

CHAPTER, PAIN IS THE SAME

16

TAMMY

I had gotten so disgusted that I went to a diner to get something to eat. But the Ruben sandwich I ordered along with a side of fries had gotten cold. Because for real, I didn't want the food. I wanted an explanation as to what was happening with my life.

After some time, I called my mother. Since we were in a different time zone, I was concerned she wouldn't answer the call. Luckily for me she did.

"Hi, mommy,"

She yawned. "I was thinking about you all day. Had a feeling you would call. Are you ok?"

I grabbed a fry and chewed it slowly. It almost tasted like wax in my mouth. "I don't know what to do anymore. I mean, I think you're right when you say there's something about madness that I love. I just wish I knew how to change. I tried moving away. Twice to be honest. But things stayed the same."

"I understand, Tammy. But you have to look at you're craving for drama as what it is. An addiction. And it's never easy to get over an addiction."

I knew she was telling the truth. But I needed more. I needed a guide or blueprint. I felt like I was getting deeper into a depressive state. And I didn't like myself in this dark place.

"I need help, Mommy. I can't do this alone. I don't even know where to start. All of the friends and all of the relationships that surround me are based in this dramatic state. So how can you pull yourself out if it's always been your life?"

"I'll tell you what I did. The first thing I did was go to rehab. And I know what you're about to say and you're right. There aren't any places available for rehab when it comes to being a dramatic person. But there should be."

I laughed.

"But I did a few other things too." She continued. "Once I got out of rehab I did move out of my environment. And I started doing things different. I read books instead of looking at TV. I took long drives instead of going to clubs or bars. I took myself out to dinner when I wanted a meal away from home. And when I felt sad, and when I felt alone, I allowed myself to cry."

"But I don't wanna cry."

"Tammy, there is nothing wrong with crying and letting your emotions go. There have been studies that holding emotions in can cause cancer. You have to like yourself first. Or no one else will like you. And the best way to do that is to feel something."

I knew she was telling the truth and she always knew what to say. So, what did a life look like without Devon? Without Jamie? Without Miracle and even Brooklyn? I don't know but I was willing to find out.

JAMIE

We were having so much fun until Tammy with her dry ass tried to ruin it all. These guys knew how to handle my body. And it made me forget how much fun I had in my freaky days. When I used to go to clubs, pick up something I liked and took it home. I think women get a bad rap who enjoy sex. But I didn't care. I like what I liked and how I liked it.

We were about to fuck again when I went to the bathroom. My pussy was so raw that I wanted to press a warm washcloth on it. I don't care how much pain I was in at the moment. We were going to go all night if I had anything to say about it.

After I finished washing up, I walked out into the room. But the door was wide open, and they were gone. My heart stopped in my chest. I immediately turned my head to the right. My purse was gone too.

Suddenly I felt so stupid.

I knew for a fact that Tammy would not let me hear the end of this. Why should she? I played myself something terrible. When I heard my phone ring I rushed to the bed. The only reason I still had it was that I slept with it most nights. Had they known it was tucked under my pillow they probably would have taken that too.

When I looked down at the number, I saw it was my husband. For some reason I answered. I flopped on the edge of the bed. "I don't feel like talking now."

"I just wanna talk to you for 5 seconds. After that I'll let you do whatever you wanna do. I promise."

"I can do whatever I want to do now!"

"That's not what I mean." He said softly.

I rolled my eyes. "Why don't you just leave me alone? I moved on with my life! Don't you get it? For the first time ever, I'm not stressed out. I'm not scared. And I don't wanna come back home. Ever!"

"I can't leave you alone." His words sounded like a threat.

"You don't have a choice."

"You're my wife. And we made vows. And I wanna honor those vows."

"I don't get it. Why care about vows now? You didn't when you beat me. Don't you understand? I remember everything!"

"I know and that's why I'm coming to you like a man."

"Brooklyn, don't you want me happy?"

"I do. I want you to lead a full life. Just not without me. I'm so sorry."

BROOKLYN

I'm not going to lie I don't care what this bitch had over me, I was tired of her blackmailing me about the kidnapping. At the end of the day she was going to do what she wanted. Even if it meant telling Penny. Still, I was driving down the street talking to her on the phone. And she was doing everything she could to get on my nerves.

"I'm confused." I said leaning deeper into my seat. "Did dude come home last night or not? Because when I left him, he said he was going straight home."

"That's how I know you don't pay me any attention. I told you he came home but he didn't sleep in our bedroom. I guess the girl I hired did her job too good. And now he feels as though he don't want to be in our bed."

"I know for a fact he not about to leave you for a stripper. So, stop worrying about everything."

"I never said he was going to leave me. I said I hired you to do a job and—"

"Hold up, you didn't hire me to do anything. What you're doing is blackmailing me. There's a difference."

"I know what I'm doing. And every day that I allow you to live is my payment to you. Along with the twenty thousand you spent. So, like I said I'm paying you to do a job and your job is to make sure that he shows up to that alter."

BY MERCEDES BISHOP

"So, you really think he's going to call off the marriage?"

"I don't know but what else could it be? I mean, he said he had to talk to me about something very important. Unless you know something I don't, I feel as though it's about our wedding."

"I need to know something straight up. Are you in love with this dude or do you have other motive's in mind? Because I've never known someone to be so pressed over a man who didn't wanna be bothered."

"I'm sorry, when did you find out he doesn't wanna be bothered?"

I made a left and merged on the highway. Trying to ask myself why I allowed her to rope me into a sentence I didn't mean. Of course, I knew he didn't wanna be bothered. He told me himself. But it didn't mean I was supposed to tell her.

"On everything I love, dude didn't tell me he didn't want to be with you anymore. I'm only basing this off of what you're saying."

"So, what you saying?" She yelled.

I swear, this girl just wanted to fight. "Aye, Miracle, it's like this. I love the both of you together. I think it's a good look. As a matter of fact, I know it is. But you can't be pressing the man so hard. Let him come to you sometimes. Let him trip off of you. Because whoever loves the other the most has the least power. And if I know you, I know you love power."

"Nigga, you don't know nothing about me. All you know is what I've told you. You don't know what I'm capable of. Because if you did you would've killed me when you had a chance. And now it's too late. Because I told at least two people what you did to me. And if I ever come up missing, they'll be coming to you first."

The moment she said that my stomach chopped. As far as I knew we were the only ones that knew, with the exception of Berkley who I was dodging.

"I promise you this, he will be marrying you. Trust me. I'll make sure he's there myself!"

"You better! Or it will be on your head."

TAMMY

I had a peaceful night sleep. After talking to my mother, I realized there were things I needed to do. Like move on with my life. But not with the crutch I have now. Jamie has got to go. So, after eating a big breakfast

BY MERCEDES BISHOP

I went back to the hotel. I had to let Jamie know that I was moving on. It may have sounded like I was bipolar. But I couldn't see things clearer if I tried.

Why? Well, after seeing how freaked out she was there was no way I could spend any more time with her. Don't get me wrong, if you're grown you should be able to do what you want. But two guys at the same time when you're getting out of a marriage is, to me, weird as fuck.

When I walked into the hotel room, I was surprised she wasn't there. She must've still been at the other room with those guys. I decided to straighten up a little before checkout. So, I packed all of my clothes and folded them up neatly on the bed. Then I placed them inside my luggage.

After I was done, I made a few phone calls. There was this apartment I was looking at back home in Maryland. I had an appointment tomorrow that I had all intentions on making. For starters I was going to fly instead of drive since it was her car. Because although I needed to be ok with hearing myself think, driving on really long trips made me go insane.

After I packed, I knew it was time to check out. So, the moment I walked outside I was shocked to see

Brooklyn sitting in front of our room in a black truck, with Jamie in the passenger seat.

Confused, I walked over to his truck and looked inside. At that time, I could see he was holding a gun. And that she looked hysterical.

"Brooklyn, what...what are you doing out here?"

"Get inside."

"I don't understand." I shrugged. "Why are you even here?"

"If I have to say it again, I'm gonna hurt you. Now get in the fucking truck."

When I looked at Jamie she looked away. I was afraid to go with them, but I had no choice. He had a gun. So, I got inside.

We were in his truck on the way back home. Except, instead of driving himself, he made Miracle do it. With her behind the steering wheel it was like riding on a roller coaster. Anytime he spoke, her hands would shake, and the wheel would jerk, which meant the car would swerve quickly left to right.

"I really wish you'd let me drive." I said calmly from the backseat.

"I don't wanna hear shit about you driving." He said. "What I wanna know is why you took my wife to a hotel in the first place?"

230   BY MERCEDES BISHOP

I frowned. "I didn't take her anywhere. She wanted to get away from you. Because she's scared. I mean look at what you're doing now. Forcing her to drive a truck while you point a gun at us."

"I'm doing this for her," he said. "I'm doing this for you too. Don't you realize how messed up in the head Devon has been since you've been gone? I mean what is this shit? You don't just up and leave every time you have a problem."

"I'm sorry, who is Devon's fiancé again? Because it's not me."

"I'm not trying to hear all that shit! You're coming home!" He looked at Jamie. "And you're coming home too. And that's the end of it!"

CHAPTER, SHAWTY DO RIGHT

17

DEVON

I had just pulled up in front of my bank when I got a call from the girl from my bachelor party. We exchanged numbers when the night ended but to be honest, I didn't think she would return my call. I hit her earlier and said if she had some free time, I was more than willing to meet up. But hours had passed without an acknowledgment, so I counted it as a 'L'. I guess I was wrong.

"I'm surprised I heard from you," she said. "I mean, I knew it took me awhile for me to hit you back but for real it's a shock."

"Why you say that? I been trying to see what's good."

"Wait, you really don't know do you?"

"I'm gonna be honest, I don't like games. So, if you have something to say get to the point."

"Ok, I'll bite. Your fiancé paid me to be with you all night. Paid me to take pictures of what we did too."

BY MERCEDES BISHOP

I quickly parked to be sure I heard her right. What kind of sleaze bucket ass shit was Miracle on? And why did she want me filmed? This was just one of the many reasons I didn't wanna make that female my wife.

"So, she paid you to do everything? I mean, I figured you got some paper, but I thought it was a gift from one of my friends."

"You can't be serious. All your friends broke. They didn't tip me or my girls all night."

I was embarrassed. I don't know if it was because of my dude's or if it was because of Miracle. Either way I was confused on a lot of things. "Ok, so if she paid you why you hit me back today? Because I like you, but I'm not about to pay for no pussy."

"I hit you because you know how to treat a woman. You didn't make me feel like a whore. You were nice and sweet, and I figured, in my mind anyway, you're one of the good ones."

I didn't know if I could believe her. "That's different."

"It's the truth. Plus, I wanted to save you because if there was ever a vicious bitch to be born it's definitely your fiancé. You don't have to believe me, but I thought you should know. She wants something from you. I just don't know what."

TAMMY

Me, and Jamie along with Brooklyn were sitting at my table. Inside my old apartment. For whatever reason, he still had the gun waving. As if he didn't know us. As if Jamie still wasn't his wife. Based on how he was acting, I was starting to believe there was a lot of truth to him kidnapping Miracle. Despite Devon believing differently.

"Now what?" I asked. "You drove us back here so what's the point of it all? Because I'm confused."

"I have a few things that you need to know." He looked at me and then Jamie before staring back at me. "I need to make clear that you will be at Devon's side. You will help him see this wedding through."

"I don't feel like going to no wedding! I don't even feel like being in this apartment. I wanted to move on with my life. Let Devon be and marry whoever the fuck he wants. Just leave me out of it."

He looked down for a moment and me and Jamie looked at each other. "I'm going to be honest about

BY MERCEDES BISHOP

something. Because at this point, I have nothing else to lose. I was involved."

I looked at him seriously. Was he really saying what I thought he was? Could he be responsible for all the pain I experienced? Let's not forget, it's because of Miracle being kidnapped that I lost Carson, whether we were meant to be or not.

"I'm not sure if I'm understanding you right. Are you actually saying that you kidnapped our own friend?"

"You heard me correctly. And because I did it, and she knows, she put me in a situation."

"She knows about this?" Jamie yelled.

"Yes. She wasn't involved though."

"What does that mean?" I asked Brooklyn.

"Let's just say I'm forced to make sure that he marries her. And he won't, if you're not there."

When I looked over at Jamie, she looked devastated. It hit me hard too, but it was hitting her harder, I could tell. She was forced to learn that her man was not only a creep but a criminal. I felt for her. I understood her more. And I was worried about her.

"I'm not understanding why me being there, at Devon's wedding is so important. To you or anybody else. He has other friends. He has other associates. Being here, to me, is something I want to escape."

For some reason as I looked at him, I could tell he was in pain. Emotional pain. What I couldn't identify was why. No matter what the reason was I wanted to be left alone.

"I don't have to explain anything more than I already have. You will do this." He looked at Jamie. "And you're coming home. No more of this running around and playing yourself like a whore. You will honor my ring."

"Even if I did," she said softly." Even if I laid in our bed, I will never accept you as my husband again."

Wow. She had guts and I respected her big time for the move.

"I don't care if you beat me." She continued. "I don't care if you hurt me. I don't even care if you kill me. I'm done with being your victim. I'm done with worrying about how you feel because I know it will impact my mood."

"Jamie, I—."

"I'm not afraid of you anymore, Brooklyn." She said cutting him off. "And I need you to understand that. You're not taking the same woman home. I'm totally different now."

236

We were all silent. And I was blown away.

"And you can stay that way now. But let's see how you feel once I've had some time with you alone."

"Brooklyn, don't do anything stupid!" I said seeing the violent expression on his face.

"You stay out of my marriage. You stay out of my business. I've given you your orders and you will see them through."

"And what if I don't do what you ask?" I asked. "What if I decide against being at the wedding? Or being Devon's friend? What could you possibly do to me at this point?"

"I don't think you would want to find out. But let me just say you seem to care a lot about Devon. What if I made him a thing of the past?"

DEVON

I was at my food truck serving a bunch of customers. There was a football game in town and with or without a permit I always posted up not too far away. Most police officers didn't know if I had a registration or not, so they left me alone. Ignorance always worked to my advantage.

I was halfway down the line when I saw Tammy standing behind one of my customers as if she were waiting to place an order. My heart thumped. Just looking at her fucked me up. It had been a week since I saw her face, but it felt like forever.

After the customer before her left I closed my window. A few people had something smart to say because they were probably hungry, but I didn't care. I needed to see what was up with my *friend*.

"I didn't think I would be seeing you for a while." I said. Damn. She was so fucking pretty.

"Are you done serving your customers? Because a few people look mad and hungry. A terrible combination to have before a game."

"I'm not thinking about them. But then again you know that already. So, what's up with you? Where have you been? I mean, I know it hasn't been long, but it feels like forever."

"I needed to get away." She shrugged.

"I hear all of that. But you don't do a nigga like that."

"I hate when you do that. You have this fucked up way of making everything about you. What about me?

What about what I've been going through? Don't you see or even care how it makes me feel too—"

"I'm done with this situation," I said cutting her off.

"What you mean you're done? I hope you're not about to say you aren't marrying Miracle."

"Even if I wasn't, what difference does it make? You and I both know I don't need to be with that girl. I was serious about wanting to take things to another level with you. I mean do you feel the same way?"

She was quiet.

"Come on, Tammy. I'm tired of playing games. We've been doing this for years. We should finally be with who we want to be with. Each other."

"I wanna tell you something but I don't know if I should."

"Hold off on telling me anything right now." I said.

"Why not?"

"I wanna take you out. Just me and you. And after everything I'll hear what you have to say. Cool?"

"I don't know about this."

"Why? Because of some bitch I don't care about? Fuck that shit, Tammy! Fuck everybody as far as I'm concerned. I'm only asking for one day. One day where we pretend we're not friends. One day where we're actually together. Can you do that for me?"

We were in a bar drunk as fuck. It was actually our third bar for the night and neither one of us wanted to go home. It's amazing when you finally realize that you can be with someone who's actually your friend. All my life I went about things the wrong way. I went after how women looked or felt while I was inside of them. But with Tammy it was a full package. She was everything to me and I hadn't even touched her.

"I like this, I mean, spending time with you alone." She admitted in a little drunk slur. "We've always had this connection but, I mean, it's hard to explain."

"You don't have to do or say anything. All you have to do is go with the flow." I said.

After a few more drinks I took a deep breath. Looking down at my watch I knew it was a matter of time before I got a hateful text message from Miracle. It was also time to hear what Tammy wanted to tell me. Although I have to admit. I wasn't in the mood.

I was where I wanted to be.

Period.

CHAPTER, HALF ON A WEDDING

18

TAMMY

I had so much fun with Devon. Like there's nothing that could compare to how giddy I felt in this moment. From the conversation we had, to the barhopping and laughing, everything was perfect. The only downside, if there's a downside at all, was having to tell him that his best friend was foul. Which I hadn't done just yet.

When it was time to leave a bar with him, I could see in his eyes he didn't wanna go home. And I didn't want to let him go. We both knew that in one day there would be a wedding whether we wanted it to be or not. Still, we parted ways.

I was just about to take a bath when my phone rang. I was blown away when I saw who was hitting me up. And yet I decided to answer anyway. "Carson?"

"I know you don't want to hear from me."

"I don't have anything against you." I sat up and the water splashed. "To be honest, I understand why you broke up with me. Being in a relationship with you was my first chance to try and do things right. And I guess I'm more immature than I thought." I laughed softly.

"I hear what you're saying. I just feel like I made a mistake."

I was shocked by what he was saying. Never in a million years would I think Carson would call me back and try to make up. I was a trash bag. I knew I was a trash bag. So, did he forget?

"I don't understand what you're saying right now." I got out of the tub and wrapped a towel around my body. "This, this doesn't sound like you." I sat on my sofa and looked out into my place.

"What don't you understand. I think I've made myself clear. You were the one who got away."

This man had to be drinking. I was the worst girlfriend ever. I would leave his house in the middle of the night to go see Devon. I would answer the phone if Devon called, leaving him on hold for hours. There was nothing about me good, except when it came to my loyalty to Devon. He had the right idea about breaking up with me. So why didn't he know that anymore?

"Carson, I'm sorry but I…I mean…I moved on."

"That quick?"

I frowned. "I don't see how you can say that. Whether I was wrong or not, you moved on way before I did remember?"

"I already know who your with too." I could hear the hate in his voice.

I raised my head. This man would not make me feel bad. "I have to go."

"This not over, bitch."

I was so shocked I dropped the phone on the couch. I don't know what he was tripping off, but he needed to quit immediately. At first, I felt bad for being dumped by him. And now I'm thinking my intuition was right. Maybe there was something way off with Carson that I couldn't see at first.

I was just about to slide on my pajamas when there was a knock at my door. My body trembled. Was he coming to beat me up or worse? Slowly I walked to my door and looked out the peephole. I was surprised to see Devon on the other side. I quickly snatched the door open before he could change his mind and walk away.

"I can't believe you're here."

"I didn't want to go home." I stared at him longer than I should have. "You gonna let me in?"

"Oh, yes…I…come in." I pulled his hand and locked the door. Standing in front of him I took a deep breath. "I don't want you to have trouble with Miracle."

"I got trouble with Miracle now." He led me to the sofa. "Listen, I'm gonna marry her based on what you said to me at the bar. And I know it goes against what we both feel."

"I don't care about you marrying her. I understand its payment for the truck. I also know how you feel about me and I know how I feel about you."

"But I want you to be my best man."

"I can't do that!" I laughed. "She would kill me!"

"I know what you're saying. But if I'm going to do this whatever this is, I need you by my side. It's the only way. Because when I'm saying my vows, I will be thinking about you. I won't mean the words to her. Do you understand?"

I didn't respond. Within seconds our lips met. I don't even know how we made it from the couch to the floor. But there we were…him on top of me kissing me softly. Looking into my eyes. Before I knew it, he found his way inside of my body. It was like I was being electrocuted with thousands of volts of pleasure. Why hadn't we been doing this before? Everybody else thought we had.

He moved slowly in and out in and out. Like he wanted to experience each moment. My legs trembled. My body warmed up. My face was red and hot to the touch. It was like we were meant to be.

"I love you," I said.

"I love you more. You are my girl. And I don't care what the fuck anybody thinks about it."

TAMMY

It was my love's wedding day. A day where I should be sad. So, tell me why as I walked out my apartment on the way to pick up my bestgirl dress, which was totally last-minute sense I wasn't in the wedding party before, I was on cloud nine?

That is until I saw who was sitting in the parking lot. Slowly I walked over to him. "I don't understand why you're in front of my house, Carson."

"I'm going to your event with you. Or did you rescind the invitation?"

"I didn't think I had to say the words. We aren't together anymore. You know it and I do too. So why would I want to take you to the wedding?"

"Don't make me say it again. Get in the fucking car."

MIRACLE

This was supposed to be a happy day for me and in some ways it was. But when Devon came home last night instead of getting in the shower he got straight into bed. When I asked him why he didn't want to clean up, he said he liked how he smelled. Fuck kind of sense does that make. I didn't let it bother me too much. As I've made my goal clear. We were getting married whether he wanted to or not.

The next morning, I was in the hotel getting ready for my big day. I had my bridesmaids around me, and everyone looked great. I always wanted to be married in this color scheme so seeing how everything played out gave me chills. Their make-up was right. Their hair was right. They lost the right amount of weight. And they were gorgeous. I'm talking sheer perfection.

BY MERCEDES BISHOP

Even Jamie who seemed to have an attitude looked the part. I was about to go to one of my friend's room, to ask her how I looked. But when I walked into the hallway and saw Tammy, I was stunned.

I rushed up to her. "What you doing here?" I asked.

"I'm in the wedding party." She shrugged.

"I'm confused. I knew you had an invitation to the event, but I don't recall inviting you in my party. I don't fuck with homewreckers."

"I didn't say I was in your party. I'm with Devon. He asked me to be his best man."

I can't explain it. I don't even know how it happened. But upon hearing those words I yanked her hard. There I was in my wedding dress fighting her like we were outside. Like we didn't have history. Like this wouldn't momentarily ruin the day. Hearing the commotion, my bridesmaids came out just as Devon and his groomsmen exited their rooms too.

Me and Tammy were still fighting while others were trying to pull us away from each other. We all got bruised. And it was pandemonium. On my wedding day.

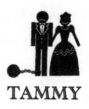

TAMMY

Don't ask me how we did it. I couldn't tell you. All I know is Devon and Miracle were officially married. Yes, people had questions. After all, when they were saying their vows earlier, we all looked as if we had been in a big fight. But in the end Devon's obligation to Miracle was officially over.

Now the next part of our plan could begin.

As the reception got underway, Devon and I looked at each other periodically at the wedding party table. Although last minute, it was my time to say a few words since I was officially his best man.

I wondered why Brooklyn didn't fight much like he did in the past when Devon told him about the change. But he seemed resigned when he told him his best man would be me. Like he didn't care. Like he was worn out. Maybe he was scared.

When I stood up to make my speech, if looks could kill, the way Miracle was staring me down, I would be dead. Take nothing from the fact that Carson, who sat with five men I didn't know, also shot daggers my way.

BY MERCEDES BISHOP

We rode together after I picked up my dress. So, when did his uninvited squad arrive?

Still, with my glass in hand, aching and bruised from the fight, I said, "I just wanna say that no matter what Devon will be happy. And for that I'm grateful."

When I made my speech, I sat down and Devon winked at me. I smiled because these people have no idea how much things would be changing.

When the music got underway Carson couldn't wait to yank me up. "I know you're up to something. What is it?"

I snatched away. "You may still feel something for me now, but let's be clear, I'm done with you. I don't owe you any explanation. You broke up with me. So, let that keep you sane at night."

"There is a lot of things about me you don't know. Perhaps if you did, you would be more cautious with how you talk to me."

"I have to go to the bathroom."

"You got fifteen minutes."

I quickly ran to the stairwell like planned. Devon was already waiting. The moment he saw my face he smiled. "What took you so long?"

"I'm here now."

I smiled brighter. "You ready to spend the rest of your life with me?"

"Ready when you are."

With that we exited the building and into our waiting car. Three hours later we boarded a plane to Arizona, where we made plans to spend the rest of our lives together.

After looking everywhere for Devon and Tammy...Miracle, Brooklyn and Carson ended up in the hallway of the hall where the reception was taking place. "Where the fuck are they?" Carson asked out of breath.

Miracle shook her head and smiled. "Wow."

"What's funny?" Brooklyn asked.

"They left." She shrugged. "They finally fucking left together. And they did it right up under our noses."

"We know that but where did they go?" Carson asked.

Just then Jamie walked out. "Did you find them?" She asked.

"Stop playing games." Brooklyn said with a lowered brow. "I know you know where they went."

They all crowded around her eager for answers. "Honestly, I don't." She shrugged. "They didn't tell me anything. I'm as shocked as you all are. But I'm glad they finally did make the move."

"Make the move of what?" Carson asked.

"To leave. Together."

"So, you do know where they went?" Brooklyn said yanking her arm.

"I'ma need you to let her go." Carson said firmly.

Brooklyn stared him down.

"Please, let her go." He said again.

He released her.

"It doesn't matter where they went." Miracle said. "Just as long as they don't mess up my plans. Because by this time next week, I'll be a very wealthy woman."

CHAPTER, SMELLS LIKE RAIN

19

DEVON

MONTHS LATER

She smelt like rain and coconut. How was that possible? Although it was pouring down outside, we had been in the house for over an hour and had gotten dried. Her smell, her presence, was the only distraction from the mess of what I had made of our lives.

I was the one who suggested we run away from it all. Prior to leaving with Tammy, we were friends. We had a life. We had moments of happiness that had nothing to do with our responsibility to each other financially.

Tammy and I had grown up together. From kids. And now I was responsible for her well-being. I wish I was the man I thought I was in my mind. The man I set out to be. But now I'm seeing that maybe that's not true.

As we sat on the floor in our one-bedroom apartment with bills surrounding us, I was heartbroken.

BY MERCEDES BISHOP

The plan was to go to the movies and get something to eat earlier in the night and we tried. Until we charged our final credit card. The one we lived off, only for it to be denied. She ended up having to tap the savings she had been given from Carson, which at this point was dwindling.

"I wish you would tell me what's on your mind." Tammy said holding the light bill. "I hate when you're like this."

"I told you I'm fine."

"You said that but it's not how you're acting."

I put the bill down and ran my hand down my face. "I mean look at our lives, Tammy. I wanted to take you out to eat and can't even do it because we don't have credit. And we can't even pay our bills."

"Are you saying you regret being with me?"

"How could you say that to me? You know how I feel about you. I just hate that I put us through this. And I would think you wouldn't wanna be with me."

"Of course, I do. And I feel in my heart that things will be ok. I mean, I know things look bad, but I know we will make a way. We always do."

"You want me to believe that you could be with a broke man?"

"I want you to believe that I can be with a man that I love. Yes, I want it different for us. Yes, I wanted us to have happily ever after. And there's nothing to say that it won't happen in the future. But I also understand that good things come to those who wait." She touched my hand. "Wait with me, Devon. Wait with me. And I promise we will be fine."

The fact that she was so optimistic made me want to fight for her even more. But I also knew the real deal. She was a woman and I was a man and it was my responsibility to take care of her. I heard the conversation she had with her mother when she thought I wasn't listening. I know her mother was concerned that we made a big mistake. After these long calls with her moms, she would go on and on about being in love with madness. Whatever that meant. Each time she talked to her mother she walked away feeling sadder.

But her mother is not alone. Everybody thought we were best friends and worse as lovers, but this was our relationship not theirs and we didn't owe anybody anything, especially not an explanation.

After we sorted out the bills that we *could* pay on her job as a waitress and my job as a short order cook, we got in bed. Holding each other while the windows were open, and the moonlight came shining inside.

But I was angry.

Furious.

Because had I been smarter and more aware that the reason that bitch wanted to marry me was due to the money my father left, we wouldn't be in this situation now.

Miracle stole over a million dollars.

A million dollars!

And it was mine.

While I was fucking with that truck business, she managed to take my inheritance in a sneaky ass move. I didn't even know he died in his sleep, months before our wedding. On the same day she claimed I asked her to be my wife.

She held onto the check. Had somebody pretend to be me and deposited the check the day after we got married. Even got Penny involved by throwing me off with the money for the trucking business. It was the same money Miracle and I took to run away. It's laughable that we thought we were getting away with something.

The whole time I was losing the big money.

I would never have known if I hadn't called the bank about my personal account I opened. They pulled up the joint account we used to share instead and mentioned the withdrawl of a million dollars. After a little investigation I found out she had been planning this for a while.

I tried to fight it with a lawyer. Even moved back to Maryland. But she pretended to be hurt because I left her for her *best friend*. That's what she told her attorney. Her best friend? She couldn't stand Tammy.

But it didn't make a difference. Her case against me was solid. I did leave the day of our wedding. That was me getting my dick sucked by a prostitute in the pictures she showed. And I never wanted to be with her.

After hearing my case, my own lawyer looked at me like an animal.

The only thing that kept Miracle alive was the promise I made to Tammy. She begged me to be calm. Said that she didn't want our love story to end with me going to jail.

So why couldn't I shake the feeling?

Irritated, I got up, slid out of bed and walked to my drawer.

"What are you doing?" Tammy asked sitting up in bed, with her back against the headboard.

I loaded my gun and placed it on the dresser before putting on my clothes. "Go back to sleep."

"I asked you a question! What are you doing?"

I raised my shirt and stuffed the gun in my waist band and walked out the door.

COMING SOON

BY MERCEDES BISHOP

CARTEL PUBLICATIONS

PRESENTS

The Cartel Publications Order Form

www.thecartelpublications.com

Inmates **ONLY** receive novels for $10.00 per book **PLUS** shipping fee **PER BOOK.**
(Mail Order **MUST** come from inmate directly to receive discount)

Shyt List 1	_____	$15.00
Shyt List 2	_____	$15.00
Shyt List 3	_____	$15.00
Shyt List 4	_____	$15.00
Shyt List 5	_____	$15.00
Shyt List 6	_____	$15.00
Pitbulls In A Skirt	_____	$15.00
Pitbulls In A Skirt 2	_____	$15.00
Pitbulls In A Skirt 3	_____	$15.00
Pitbulls In A Skirt 4	_____	$15.00
Pitbulls In A Skirt 5	_____	$15.00
Victoria's Secret	_____	$15.00
Poison 1	_____	$15.00
Poison 2	_____	$15.00
Hell Razor Honeys	_____	$15.00
Hell Razor Honeys 2	_____	$15.00
A Hustler's Son	_____	$15.00
A Hustler's Son 2	_____	$15.00
Black and Ugly	_____	$15.00
Black and Ugly As Ever	_____	$15.00
Ms Wayne & The Queens of DC **(LGBT)**	_____	$15.00
Black And The Ugliest	_____	$15.00
Year Of The Crackmom	_____	$15.00
Deadheads	_____	$15.00
The Face That Launched A Thousand Bullets	_____	$15.00
The Unusual Suspects	_____	$15.00
Paid In Blood	_____	$15.00
Raunchy	_____	$15.00
Raunchy 2	_____	$15.00
Raunchy 3	_____	$15.00
Mad Maxxx (4th Book Raunchy Series)	_____	$15.00
Quita's Dayscare Center	_____	$15.00
Quita's Dayscare Center 2	_____	$15.00
Pretty Kings	_____	$15.00
Pretty Kings 2	_____	$15.00
Pretty Kings 3	_____	$15.00
Pretty Kings 4	_____	$15.00
Silence Of The Nine	_____	$15.00

YOU LEFT ME NO CHOICE   259

Silence Of The Nine 2	_____	$15.00
Silence Of The Nine 3	_____	$15.00
Prison Throne	_____	$15.00
Drunk & Hot Girls	_____	$15.00
Hersband Material **(LGBT)**	_____	$15.00
The End: How To Write A	_____	$15.00
Bestselling Novel In 30 Days (Non-Fiction Guide)		
Upscale Kittens	_____	$15.00
Wake & Bake Boys	_____	$15.00
Young & Dumb	_____	$15.00
Young & Dumb 2: Vyce's Getback	_____	$15.00
Tranny 911 **(LGBT)**	_____	$15.00
Tranny 911: Dixie's Rise **(LGBT)**	_____	$15.00
First Comes Love, Then Comes Murder	_____	$15.00
Luxury Tax	_____	$15.00
The Lying King	_____	$15.00
Crazy Kind Of Love	_____	$15.00
Goon	_____	$15.00
And They Call Me God	_____	$15.00
The Ungrateful Bastards	_____	$15.00
Lipstick Dom **(LGBT)**	_____	$15.00
A School of Dolls **(LGBT)**	_____	$15.00
Hoetic Justice	_____	$15.00
KALI: Raunchy Relived	_____	$15.00
(5th Book in Raunchy Series)		
Skeezers	_____	$15.00
Skeezers 2	_____	$15.00
You Kissed Me, Now I Own You	_____	$15.00
Nefarious	_____	$15.00
Redbone 3: The Rise of The Fold	_____	$15.00
The Fold (4th Redbone Book)	_____	$15.00
Clown Niggas	_____	$15.00
The One You Shouldn't Trust	_____	$15.00
The WHORE The Wind		
Blew My Way	_____	$15.00
She Brings The Worst Kind	_____	$15.00
The House That Crack Built	_____	$15.00
The House That Crack Built 2	_____	$15.00
The House That Crack Built 3	_____	$15.00
The House That Crack Built 4	_____	$15.00
Level Up **(LGBT)**	_____	$15.00
Villains: It's Savage Season	_____	$15.00
Gay For My Bae	_____	$15.00
War	_____	$15.00
War 2: All Hell Breaks Loose	_____	$15.00
War 3: The Land Of The Lou's	_____	$15.00
War 4: Skull Island	_____	$15.00
War 5: Karma	_____	$15.00
War 6: Envy	_____	$15.00
War 7: Pink Cotton	_____	$15.00
Madjesty vs. Jayden (Novella)	_____	$8.99
You Left Me No Choice	_____	$15.00

(**Redbone 1** & **2** are **NOT** Cartel Publications novels and if **ordered** the cost is **FULL** price of $15.00 **each**. **No Exceptions**.)

Please add **$5.00** for shipping and handling fees for up to **(2) BOOKS PER ORDER**. (INMATES INCLUDED) (See next page for details)

The Cartel Publications * P.O. BOX 486 OWINGS MILLS MD 21117

Name: _____

Address: _____

City/State: _____

Contact/Email: _____

Please allow 8-10 BUSINESS days Before shipping.

PLEASE NOTE DUE TO <u>COVID-19</u> SOME ORDERS MAY TAKE UP TO 3 WEEKS BEFORE THEY SHIP

The Cartel Publications is <u>NOT</u> responsible for <u>Prison Orders</u> rejected!

<u>NO RETURNS and NO REFUNDS</u>
<u>NO PERSONAL CHECKS ACCEPTED</u>
<u>STAMPS NO LONGER ACCEPTED</u>

CPSIA information can be obtained
at www.ICGtesting.com
Printed in the USA
LVHW031630090720
660247LV00003B/427